"Would you have kissed me willingly?"

Thorne's mild question irritated Addie.

"Can you ask that with a straight face?" she countered. "A kiss is a token of affection. Affection is the last thing I feel for you!"

"Well, there you have it." He slapped the steering wheel lightly. "It had to be done."

She stared at him. "*Had* to be done?"

"Miriam would have been disappointed if you'd come home with lipstick intact."

Addie gritted her teeth in frustration. "Miriam!" she threw at him. "Don't pretend you kissed me just for her!"

"Very well, I won't." His smile was maddening. "As long as you don't pretend you didn't want it, too."

Virginia Hart comes from a family of writers. Her sister writes mysteries, and her husband—who's even more romantic than Virginia's "heroes"—is an award-winning country-music songwriter. Virginia, not to be outdone, has written mysteries, historical romances, Westerns, and now Harlequin Romances. Confusion is the order of the day at the Harts' Burbank, California, home, with Virginia at her typewriter, cola in hand—she says she's addicted—and her husband composing and singing at the top of his lungs. Their two sons, no doubt, add to the creative chaos.

Books by Virginia Hart

HARLEQUIN ROMANCE
2811—SWEET PRETENDER
2882—NIGHT OF THE SPRING MOON
2980—WITHOUT RAINBOWS

LOVE OR MONEY
Virginia Hart

Harlequin Books

TORONTO • NEW YORK • LONDON
AMSTERDAM • PARIS • SYDNEY • HAMBURG
STOCKHOLM • ATHENS • TOKYO • MILAN

ISBN 0-373-03135-1

Harlequin Romance first edition July 1991

LOVE OR MONEY

CHAPTER ONE

As if propelled by the sudden rush of chill wind that lifted her fawn-colored hair and sent silky threads of it flying every which way, Addie Rutherford took the porch steps two at a time and burst into the living room.

"Brrr! Whoever said it doesn't get cold in Southern California?"

"Somebody who never lived here. Shut the dang door!" her grandfather barked, hunching over to shield the pieces of the giant jigsaw puzzle he'd been working on for most of the week. "I'm finally getting the outline of this chocolate bar."

"Chocolate bar!" Addie scoffed, shrugging her slender shoulders out of the fake fur jacket that exactly matched the rich amber of her eyes. "Whatever became of scenic meadows, seascapes and cuddly kittens as subjects for jigsaw puzzles?"

"This kind is more of a challenge."

"I see. And the puzzle hasn't been devised that can lick Barney Rutherford," she teased, mimicking the clench-toothed way he had of boasting.

"You've got that right, little girl."

She crossed the room and stood behind him to press her lips to the shiny place on his scalp that he covered strategically with strands of silver-gray hair. "Aha! That piece doesn't fit—it's too dark a brown. See?" She pointed.

He shivered free of the cold fingers that brushed his. "You're a walking icicle. Hop out of those clothes and into something comfortable. The stew's ready and waiting."

"Mmm. Don't I know it." She inhaled deeply as she scurried toward her room. "A mob is forming outside, preparing to break in for a taste."

"Let 'em come. There's plenty."

She had to smile at that. Her grandfather was proud of his cooking, and rightly so. Besides, he loved company. Just about anyone was welcome to share one of his delicious meals—and pay for it by sitting on the couch, looking through endless stacks of photograph albums and listening to stories of the good old days.

"A letter came for you," he called as she was smoothing her favorite khaki fatigue pants over her hips. "It's from a Miriam Rutherford Mandeville—if that isn't a name and a half? Who is she?"

With a groan, Addie pulled the sleeves of her cocoa-brown sweater down to cover her wrists and adjusted the gold chain of her watch band. Darn it. She hadn't counted on Barney's getting to the mailbox first. He closed the hardware store promptly at three every day. By the time he got home and started dinner, it was after four. Then he always worked on his current jigsaw puzzle and became too absorbed in it to think about the postman.

"Who is she?" he persisted.

"A woman I know. Did you fix a salad?"

"You don't need anything but a spoon and a healthy appetite for my stew. It's a garden in a pot." He squinted at her as she came back into the room, her hair parted neatly in the center now, and brushed satiny smooth to glide over her shoulders and frame her heart-shaped face.

"Is the Rutherford part of this woman's name only a coincidence?"

"As a matter of fact, it isn't."

Darn, darn, darn. There had never been lies between her and Barney, not even little "white" ones. A lie was a lie according to his code. And he wasn't just her grandfather, he was her dearest friend.

They'd grown close ever since her father had accepted the promotion that swept him and Addie's mother and younger brother to London, England. Addie was in the middle of her first semester at Loma Linda University then. She would have been badgered unmercifully to give up her own plans, and go with them, if Barney hadn't stood at her side, arguing with equal force that she should be allowed to decide her own future and follow her own dreams.

He and Addie would be responsible for each other, he insisted. Recently a widower, he'd explained that the arrangement would be to his advantage, as well as Addie's.

"A man needs at least part of his family beside him in his twilight years."

It was the "twilight years" part that had brought tears to her mother's eyes, and Addie had been allowed to stay without being made to feel guilty.

"She calls you 'Adeline,'" Barney growled, holding the envelope at arm's length and peering at it over the top of his rimless glasses.

"My name *is* Adeline," she reminded him, bustling around the table, folding napkins and clattering silver in the hope of distracting the elderly man from his inevitable questions. "Let's use the good china bowls tonight, shall we?"

"Adelines have aristocratic noses. Narrow straight ones. Not ones that tilt up at the end. And definitely not ones that're covered with freckles." He got up and came toward her, waving the envelope. "Well, who is she?"

It was no use. Addie pressed a finger to a spot between her eyebrows, as if the action would help her concentrate. "Miriam is—let me see—your great-grandfather's nephew's granddaughter."

He blinked. "My what?"

Over delicious spoonfuls of stew, she explained about the mountains of research she'd been doing for almost a year, fitting together a puzzle of another sort. The Rutherford family tree. She had planned to assemble everything and present it to her grandfather for his seventy-third birthday in July.

He needed something to keep his spirits up. Only a few months ago, his partner of thirty-five years, who'd supposedly been in excellent health, had suffered a sudden stroke and died while arguing with a customer about the cost of repairing a waffle iron.

If the loss of this old and dear friend wasn't bad enough, now he was in danger of losing the store.

The partner's son and heir wanted to sell the business. He was willing to wait a reasonable length of time for Barney to arrange financing to buy his share. So far, Barney hadn't been able to come up with the money.

Although the books showed that the store was doing well, no lending institution he'd approached was willing to take a chance on a man his age.

With characteristic optimism, he'd chuckled and said he was far from licked. A man didn't stay in the hardware business as long as he had without building a good reputation. It would be a snap to find someone willing to invest in a thriving store. He'd probably be able to pick and choose investors. But secretly, Addie knew, he was worried.

She'd hoped that the work she'd done on the family tree would cheer him. It was supposed to be a surprise, but now the proverbial cat was out of the bag.

Barney was an avid believer in people, in family and in the history of those who'd tramped the road of life before him. While his mother's line had been traced to fifteenth-century Cornwall, the Rutherford side came to an abrupt halt with a paternal grandfather, who'd been born in Chicago, Illinois, and orphaned at the age of ten. The Great Fire of 1871 had wiped out so many government records that Addie's letters of inquiry and requests for earlier documents—birth certificates, deeds, marriage licenses—had been futile.

But Addie had come across a wonderful genealogical library on Santa Monica Boulevard, only a few blocks from the hospital where she worked. Here were thousands of rolls of microfilm and floor-to-ceiling shelves of intriguing volumes.

It was hard work. Hordes of Rutherfords roamed the earth, it seemed, and she'd run into one blind alley after another, attempting to establish some kind of link. When she'd almost decided to give up, she found it, and squealed loudly in delight.

In the history of Cook County, she discovered a notation about Isaiah Rutherford, who had been disinherited by his father because he'd chosen to remain in Boston when the rest of the family moved to Illinois. Census reports verified his existence, and an obituary in an old newspaper furnished names and addresses of his son Isaiah junior's surviving relatives. Telephone directories provided addresses for some of those relatives, and one—Miriam—had answered Addie's letter.

Like a small boy overwhelmed by his gifts on Christmas morning, Barney spread out all the material she'd gathered on the coffee table, chuckling to himself. He kept up an enthusiastic commentary, not realizing and maybe not caring, that she couldn't hear him over the clatter she made washing the dishes.

"Cousin Miriam wants you to come for a visit, does she?" he called, rereading one of the letters.

"Yes. I think she's been terribly lonesome since she was widowed a year and a half ago."

"Going to fly there on your vacation?"

Addie poured two cups of hot chocolate, dropped a marshmallow in each, and set her grandfather's to one side of the table, where he wouldn't knock it over in his excitement. "You and I are planning to visit Becky and her family then, remember?"

"Your sister and her husband were here at Christmas," he argued. "Besides, I'm not crazy about listening to another lecture on how it's time I started thinking about retirement. I always feel like I'm a hundred and ten when I finally leave."

"They mean well. They just don't know how much the store means to you," Addie told him.

"Anyway, we can drive up to Oregon anytime. It isn't that far. Nope. I want you to accept this woman's invitation. It's the opportunity of a lifetime. She's even offering to send you an airline ticket."

"I know. Naturally I can't accept it. But isn't it nice of her? She's been running her husband's candy store since his death, and even though she doesn't complain, I can tell it's been a struggle for her."

Barney snatched up his cup of chocolate, then replaced it without taking a sip. "Dang it, honey, this is family. Let me spring for the fare."

Slipping off her shoes and tucking her long shapely legs under her, Addie settled beside him with her own cup. Her briefcase sat in the corner, bulging with work she'd planned to do that night. But it would have to wait. "You know it isn't a question of money. I have some saved."

"Think I can't survive without your mothering for a few weeks? I'll remember my blood-pressure pills and my vitamins."

"It isn't that."

"Then what? The business about the store? You trusted me when you were a little girl. Did something happen to change that? Have I ever let you down?"

Addie pressed her lips together. "Of course not. Everyone needs moral support. I just want to be here."

"And I want you there—representing our side of the family." He picked up a plastic-encased drawing and studied it under a magnifying glass. "Think this coat of arms is the genuine article? A lot of 'em are frauds, you know."

"Miriam said it was verified."

"Hmm. What about family pictures? Doesn't she have any?"

"She has a trunkful. But she doesn't trust them out of her sight long enough to have them copied. She's afraid they might get lost or damaged."

"Can't say I blame her. There's nothing like pictures." He put the magnifying glass down with a clatter. "Well, that's that! I'll never know what old Isaiah and the others looked like if you don't go. You have to, or this is only half a birthday present. Take that fancy camera you've been making payments on for the last two years. The one with the macro lens that does everything but whistle Yankee-Doodle. You could get copies of those pictures, easy, couldn't you, without taking 'em out of the house?''

"Yes, I could. But—"

"And take my tape recorder while you're at it. You'll capture a lot of family stories that haven't been written down anywhere."

"Oh, Grandfather," Addie sighed. Until that moment, the trip to Boston had been only a vague, maybe-someday thing. Now it was real and imminent and she wasn't sure she wanted it. Though Miriam's letters were wonderfully warm and friendly, considering the short time they'd been corresponding, she hardly knew the woman.

But it wasn't just that. And it wasn't just Barney and the store. There was Frank, as well. Her relationship with him was over. Yet not entirely. The two of them still got together now and then for coffee, and they talked regularly on the telephone. But while her heart knew they wouldn't find a way to work things out—she'd never be able to trust him again—she wasn't quite ready to put so many miles between them. It wasn't all that easy to erase nearly two years of togetherness.

"Who's this Thorne Cameron she keeps mentioning in her letters?" Barney asked, reading again. "Is he a relative, too?"

Addie cleared her throat, using the pause to wrench her thoughts away from the regrets of her past. "Not exactly. But she's known him for years and he's like a son to her."

Barney chuckled. "Sounds to me like she's dangling him in front of your nose like a carrot."

"Sounds that way to me, too," she agreed. "Miriam seems to be something of a matchmaker. According to her, Mr. Cameron is tall, extremely handsome, successful and fun to be with. He's Santa Claus and your latest movie idol in a single package, and what's more, he's unattached and dying to meet me.''

"How old is this paragon?"

"Thirty-six, I believe she said."

Barney pulled at his ear. "Thirty-six and unmarried? I don't know. A man gets too set in his ways by then to be good husband material."

"Husband material?" Now Addie had to laugh. "You're worse than Miriam. I'm not looking for a husband."

"Of course you are," he countered, staring her down.

"Not actively, in any case."

"Then again, you can't fault a man for being choosy in today's crazy world, can you? Heck, a girl came in the store this morning with green hair. Bright green! Sticking out in all directions like she'd just had the fright of her life. And the worst of it was, she was pretty. She even smiled and wished me a nice day."

Addie giggled at the picture of that encounter and of the astonished look her grandfather would have had on his face. "You can get hairsprays in all colors now, but they wash out."

"Hmph!" He picked up Miriam's letter again. "He's a lawyer, is he? Maybe getting to know this Cameron character might help you get over what's-his-name."

What's-his-name was Frank, whom Barney had never liked. According to her grandfather, a man who wouldn't even attempt to fit a piece or two into a jigsaw puzzle while he waited wasn't to be trusted.

"Grandfather! You promised—"

"Okay." He held up a flat palm. "I won't mention what's-his-name, if you stop calling me Grandfather. When you do, you really sound like an Adeline."

"It's a deal."

"Anyway, let's not talk about it anymore." He stood up and stretched. "I see you brought work home again and I don't want you sitting up all night doing it. I want you bright-eyed and beautiful when the Santa Monica Rutherfords meet the Boston Rutherfords."

"You make that sound like Frankenstein meets the Wolfman."

"Could be. Who knows what you'll find when you shake the family tree?" When he leaned over to collect his nightly kiss, he held the accompanying hug longer than usual. "Thanks, baby. For all the backbreaking research you did. It's appreciated."

"My pleasure," she said softly.

"Just think about that trip to Boston. I won't try to influence you anymore one way or the other. It's your decision one hundred percent. I've lived this long without even knowing about the East Coast Rutherfords. I can live a little longer without knowing what they look like."

No. He wouldn't try to influence her, she thought, as she watched him move toward the bathroom for his bedtime shower, favoring his left leg as he often did when he'd been sitting too long. He didn't have to try. He'd already won the argument—and he knew it.

CHAPTER TWO

IN HER LETTER to Miriam, Addie had described herself as tall and slender, with brown hair fastened into a convenient swirl at the nape of her neck. She would be wearing a biscuit-colored sweater-dress with a double strand of brown and ivory beads, and carrying an oversize brown handbag.

As she was dressing for her flight, however, she decided unhappily that the outfit, though an expensive, well-cut castoff from her sister, Becky, was colorless, and not terribly becoming. Becky's figure was not only slim, but model-straight, and on her, the dress hung without clinging. But when Addie wore it, the stretchy fabric sought out her curves and emphasized them. Had she put on a few pounds without realizing it? Had she been wrong in describing herself as slender?

Well, it was too late to make any wardrobe changes now, if the two women were going to find each other in the crowd at Logan Airport.

Miriam was, according to her own letter, "scrawny," with large hazel eyes set in too narrow a face. Her white hair was short and frizzy from an unfortunate permanent wave, and she'd be wearing shades of rose and pink—her favorite colors.

As she moved along the sloping walkway toward the people waiting expectantly for the flight's arrival, Addie spotted the woman immediately. But it wasn't Miriam herself who caught her attention. It was the man standing at her side.

Thorne Cameron. It could be no one else. She hadn't expected him to be there, but he was, and he was everything Miriam had claimed. Tall and rangy, with a firm chin, but not too firm. A prominent nose, but not too prominent. He had crisp black hair and a generous perfectly defined mouth. His deep set blue eyes could only be described as disturbing—but that made them no less attractive. They were the eyes of a man who made quick, firm decisions.

He wore an off-white zippered jacket, charcoal slacks and a knit shirt in a deep wine, which suited his coloring.

Of course, Miriam would have been too discreet to let the man know she was playing Cupid. Or would she? Addie felt like a mail-order bride, being given the once-over by the man who'd plunked down a bag of gold dust to avail himself of female companionship.

"Adeline," Miriam squealed, squeezing her escort's arm and bobbing up and down in her enthusiasm. "Oh, my darling, you are gorgeous. Isn't she adorable, Thorne?"

"She's lovely." He reached for Addie's hand with such deliberation that she wondered for a moment if he planned to kiss it. "Adeline," he repeated, giving her name a whole new sound, and she didn't tell him, as she normally would, that everyone called her Addie.

Deep and resonant, but not studiedly so, his was a nice voice. He'd said she was lovely. But then, what else could he say? He could hardly grimace and turn thumbs-down.

His car was a sporty model, blunt-nosed and gray, of a make she didn't recognize. As there was hardly enough room to accommodate two in the front, Miriam, over

Addie's protests, insisted on riding in the narrow back seat.

"I don't want to have to keep turning around," she explained, "when I want to say something to you."

The size of the car encouraged familiarity, to say the least, and Addie's senses were sharply awakened by the scent of Thorne's after-shave. More than just a pleasant scent, it was faintly stirring in the closeness of the car. She found herself trying to identify it. A hint of leather and—

Stop it! she berated herself, discomfited by the road her thoughts were taking. She didn't even know this man. Here she was in Boston. She was supposed to be noting cobbled streets, gas lamps and historical markers.

To add to the problem, being squeezed against him made her acutely aware of each movement of his thigh muscles as he applied the brakes or pressed the accelerator. And this was rush hour—stop-and-go traffic meant such movements were constant.

On the other hand, manipulations for a turn—either right or left—caused his jacketed arm to rub against hers. There shouldn't have been anything sexy about rubbing arms, so why did it unsettle her?

Had the flight been a tedious one? Miriam wanted to know. Was the airline food bearable?

They were the same questions people routinely asked anyone who'd just come off a plane, and Addie answered them easily. More original and more probing were the questions Mr. Cameron asked, though they were unspoken ones, only glittering in his eyes each time he looked at her. They gave her the curious sensation that she and Thorne were fellow conspirators, that they'd known each other for a long time and shared a secret.

"Are you sure you can only stay two weeks?" Miriam asked. "Couldn't you stretch it to a month?"

"No. I only get two weeks for my vacation," Addie told her. "A pleasure trip like this one couldn't qualify for an emergency leave of absence."

"But there's so much to see and do here. It'll take you longer than that just to do the touristy things."

"It *is* a beautiful city," Addie agreed, forcing her gaze away from Thorne Cameron's chiseled profile, and out of the window toward the glowing skyline and the shimmering lights that dappled the dark surface of the Charles River. "I've read loads of guidebooks since I decided to come here, and I'd love to stay on. But I can't."

She explained about Barney and his tendency to let things go when left to his own devices, and about her job at the hospital as a medical-records technician.

"It sounds horribly dull," Miriam pronounced.

"I love it," Addie assured her, explaining how important it was to keep accurate and complete records, not only for the sake of the patients, but also for the community, by helping to detect disease patterns.

Miriam didn't seem convinced. She probably pictured Addie shivering in a basement somewhere, going through dusty files by the light of a flickering candle.

So far, Thorne had said very little. It was impossible to tell if he was actually quiet and reserved, or if Miriam's friendly chatter allowed him no room to get a word in edgewise. That was the most likely. He was an attorney, and no attorney Addie had ever met could be accused of shyness. Becky's husband, for one, considered himself an authority on everything and seized the slightest opportunity to show it.

Barely past the center of town and before she'd had a chance to believe she was really in Boston, they pulled into a driveway and stopped. Thorne leaped out of the car, and moved around it to open the door and help them out.

Here? This couldn't be their destination. Miriam's house? Hardly. Addie had read that the owners of many of these elegant old homes had moved to the suburbs, when the upkeep became too expensive, allowing their former residences to be divided into condos. But the rents would have been enormous. Besides, large as this particular house was, it still seemed to be a single-family dwelling.

Sitting squarely behind a black iron fence that enclosed its neat square yard was a sprawling three-story gray stone mansion, with marble steps, fluted columns and violet-tinged windows. The door flew open and a dark-uniformed man greeted them briskly before taking Addie's suitcases from the car.

Inside, Addie could see a dazzling crystal chandelier, a curving stairway carpeted in soft rose, and a smiling young woman in a trim gray uniform.

"Is something wrong, Adeline?" Miriam asked, concerned.

Addie had been visualizing a cramped second-story flat, with only a couch or a cot providing extra sleeping space; whatever it was, though, it would be hers, she'd decided. No matter how the woman argued, she wouldn't allow Miriam to give up her bed. But reality was so different from what she'd imagined, she found herself speechless.

"Adeline?" Miriam looked at her quizzically.

"It's...beautiful," Addie managed. "But in your letters, you said you'd had to give up your home."

"Yes. I closed the house in Falmouth after George died. He and I had so many good times there, I couldn't bear to stay on alone. It's lovely this time of year, but, well, it's better for you in town, anyway. So much of Boston must be seen on foot, and it wouldn't be convenient for you to make the drive from Cape Cod every time you wanted to see something."

"But . . ." The protest rose in her throat and remained there as the older woman took her arm and ushered her inside.

Conscious of Thorne's following close behind, she allowed herself to be led to a huge room at the end of a long brightly lit corridor.

In spite of its size, the room was cozy and comfortable, with white wicker furniture and pale pink woodwork. Needlepoint carpets lay here and there on the polished wood floor, and the silk lamp shades were of a deeper pink. It would be even more pleasant by day, Addie thought, with the sun streaming through the fanlight windows.

"We call this the music room because of the piano," Miriam said. "Though no one plays." She sat on the couch and motioned Addie to join her.

It might have been more polite to force aside her questions and accept this unexpected reality, but Addie just couldn't. "Didn't you write me that your husband ran a neighborhood candy store?"

"So he did." Miriam adjusted one of her hairpins to better control a stray curl. "When we were first married. Then there were two stores, four, six…until now, I've lost track of how many."

"Mandeville Chocolates!" Addie cried, putting the name together with the famous company that was known on the West Coast primarily through its catalog. The candy was extremely expensive. She'd tasted it only once, when a visiting bigwig presented the staff in her department with a box to share at Christmas. "You're *that* Mandeville?"

"You didn't know?" The older woman raised a hand to her lips, laughing, as Addie explained how some of the comments in Miriam's letters had made it appear she was having a struggle financially. "Imagine that, Thorne. My darling came expecting to have to spell me behind the counter, dispensing gumdrops."

"It must be quite a surprise," he said, in a voice so flat it caught Addie's attention. The flinty eyes were faintly accusing and the lips she had thought so attractive were stretched into a tight smile. He glanced at his watch. "I'll run along now."

"Nonsense," Miriam said. "Wait here. I'll have Teresa bring tea and some of those iced cakes you like so much." Before he could argue more strongly, the elderly woman was gone.

Being naturally gregarious, Addie wasn't usually troubled by a lack of something to say. Strangers were never strangers for long. Yet she felt oddly uncomfortable with Mr. Cameron, who was clearly here against his will and resenting it. Why? Only *he* could answer that—and probably would in his own good time.

He was no less attractive for his ill humor, though had she been a mail-order bride, she would probably have taken the next stagecoach back where she'd come from.

Probably. But maybe not.

When he sat down to wait for Miriam's return, he chose the chair directly across from Addie and made no effort to hide the fact that he was studying her. Perhaps he was a bit myopic, which would account for the penetrating look in his eyes. They were nice eyes, nonetheless, with a thick brush of long straight lashes that defined them and made their blue more intense.

His wasn't a Conan the Barbarian sort of build. His muscles hadn't come from long, useless hours of weight-lifting. But even through the lined bulk of his jacket, she could tell they were the muscles of a hard-working man who led a busy active life. There was an impatience in his every move, even in his stance. Waiting didn't come easy for him.

Asking if he'd read any good books lately or if he thought it might rain would have sounded trite. What then? Thorne Cameron. With a name like that he must be of Scottish descent. She was about to remark on it, when he broke the silence.

"I hope you have some sensible shoes in those suit-cases," he said, indicating with the flick of his fingers the backless high-heeled slippers she wore. "You won't cover much ground on those stilts."

She smiled. His observation wasn't terribly friendly, but it was a start. "Oh, yes. I know what sight-seeing entails."

"I'm sure you and Miriam will want to talk the night away, but I suggest you turn in early. I have some calls to make in the morning, but they shouldn't take long. I'll be here at nine."

"You?"

"Me." He almost smiled.

Now she knew the reason for his antagonism. He was a busy man, and Miriam had pressed him into service as a tour guide. Addie could appreciate how he felt, though he might have been more civil about it. People who come to Los Angeles always expect to be taken to Disneyland, Mann's Chinese Theatre and to the La Brea Tar Pits, never realizing that living there, you might be bored with those things.

"It's kind of you to offer, Thorne," she said. "But it isn't necessary to give up your time. I've made an itinerary and—"

"Can we dispense with the polite protests?" he interrupted, beating a rat-a-tat-tat on the carved wooden chair arm with his fingers. "As I said, I'd like to be on our way by nine."

Her burst of surprised laughter sounded artificial even to her. "I have nothing to say about it?"

"No more than I have."

Oof. Was that an insult? Maybe not. Just as people dressed differently in different parts of the country, they might have different ideas of humor, though she didn't care much for his. Especially since he'd waited until Miriam was out of earshot to put it to use.

"You have plenty to say about it," she corrected. "And so do I."

If he heard her comment, he chose to ignore it. He leaned forward. "So you didn't know Miriam was well-fixed."

"Well-fixed?" she repeated, emphasizing the expression the way he had.

"So it was a coincidence that you began writing to Miriam only weeks after all those magazine stories and newspaper articles appeared on the stands."

"What articles?"

"Articles about the Mandeville family and the fiftieth anniversary of the first Mandeville Chocolates store."

"If there were such stories, I didn't see them. But I'd love to, if Miriam has extra copies."

"I'm sure she has."

He didn't believe her. He actually thought, well, she wasn't sure exactly what he thought. "I try to keep up with current news," she told him quietly. "But it isn't easy. I don't have a lot of time."

He snapped his fingers. "That's right. You work in a hospital to support yourself and your grandfather."

His timing was very good. He knew exactly where to pause and when to drop his voice. Addie flushed with embarrassment. "Don't make me sound like the Little Match Girl," she snapped. "I make a fairly good salary and Barney has his own business."

Before he could reply, Miriam was back, followed by the maid, Teresa, carrying tea and cakes. Unaware of the charged atmosphere, the older woman bustled about, moving knickknacks off the glass-topped table to make room for the tray.

"Oh, my." She pressed the back of her hand to her mouth. "Thorne doesn't drink tea. I always forget. It's coffee, strong enough to dissolve the cup. Teresa, dear, would you—"

"Don't bother." He unfolded his length into a standing position. "I have to go. I've got a mountain of work waiting."

"Tonight?" Miriam frowned for a moment, obviously wondering if she should be peevish and insist that he stay. Instead, she offered her cheek for a kiss. "I understand. I'm sure Adeline does, too.

"Isn't he absolutely perfect?" Miriam wanted to know when he'd gone.

"He's very attractive." Addie busied herself pouring the tea, hoping she wouldn't be forced into a lie.

"You'd think he'd be spoiled from so much female attention. Heads do turn when he comes into a courtroom. But he's always exactly the same way he was tonight. Sweet and unaffected."

Clearly Miriam didn't know the man as well as she thought she did. If he had his own law practice and had managed to snag the Mandeville Chocolates account, he would have made a great deal of money handling her affairs. So, why wouldn't he put his best foot forward and be nice to her? Or if he was low man on some firm's totem pole, dealing with Miriam's visiting niece would have fallen to him. Or maybe they drew straws and he lost.

"He must be a busy man," Addie said gently, still smarting from his treatment of her. "I'm not comfortable with his taking time away from his law practice to show me the sights."

"Thorne works exclusively for the company. His practice *is* Mandeville Chocolates. Besides that, he lives here. He isn't going out of his way at all."

"Here? But he said he had to leave."

"He left, but he didn't." Miriam nodded in one direction, then the other. "When my husband's health began to fail, Thorne moved into the apartment over the carriage house, wanting to be close by in case we needed him. Later, though he'd never admit it, he stayed on because of a promise he made to George to watch over me."

It was worse than Addie had imagined. Not only would she have to put up with Thorne's unpleasantness all the next day, chances were good he'd be taking meals in the main house during much of her visit.

"If you wouldn't mind, I'd rather stay home with you tomorrow," she tried, not quite ready for so much togetherness. "We have an incredible amount of catching up to do."

"You believe I'd let you stay cooped up in this old house after you wrote me about history being your passion?" Miriam waggled a forefinger. "No, indeed. You said you were looking forward to seeing Boston, and you're going to see it. We'll have plenty of time to talk.''

That was that. As Thorne had graciously put it, neither he nor Addie had anything to say about the arrangements.

After she called Barney collect to let him know she'd arrived safely, she and Miriam dug out the photographs, and as the woman had written, there was a trunkful. For Addie, whose interest in family lore had grown almost obsessive over the past few months, it was like finding a treasure chest. Before long she was able to forget the disagreeable feeling of being cross-examined by Miriam's ''perfect'' young man.

Her grandfather was going to be ecstatic, she thought later as she prepared for bed. Should she tell him about the wonderful photographs the next time she called, or should she wait and surprise him with all the copies she'd make before returning home?

As most of the house was done in rose, she was pleasantly surprised to find her room decorated in yellow—her favorite color—from the flower-sprigged wallpaper to the handsome quilt and the velvet pad on the window seat.

When, without thinking, she brought out her yellow batiste nightgown, she had to smile. It reminded her of an old movie musical, where the sets were color-coordinated with what the star was wearing.

From the window, she could see the peaked roof of what was probably the carriage house. There was a light in one of the upstairs windows. Perfumed breezes tickled her nose as she stood for long moments looking at a lovely old pear tree in full blossom.

If this *were* an old movie, she would begin singing now, as she thought about the handsome hero she'd just met. He'd be standing in the garden below, thinking about her, too, and when he heard her voice, he'd join in on the chorus.

The idea of Thorne singing a serenade to her when he'd rather run her out of town on a rail made her smile again.

Thoughts of the next morning sobered her quickly, however. Despite everything, she found herself attracted to him, and it wasn't only his striking appearance. She'd met plenty of handsome men, and she hadn't found any of them as compelling as he was. Come to think of it, she hadn't given a thought to Frank since she'd arrived.

Wouldn't it be more fair to reserve her judgment of Thorne? Given the circumstances, why shouldn't he suspect her of being an interloper bent on fleecing her newly discovered aunt? She'd have two weeks to make him rethink his prejudices and see her as she really was. They might even become friends.

"If someone gives you a lemon," Barney always said, "make lemonade."

While in high school, she'd worked in the complaints office of a large department store. Often she'd made a game out of turning the more disagreeable customers around, so they'd leave with a smile. Eight out of ten times, she'd succeeded. Thorne wasn't exactly a lemon, but he was a challenge, and since when had Barney Rutherford's granddaughter run away from a challenge?

Come the dawn, she'd be ready.

CHAPTER THREE

SHE HADN'T EXPECTED to sleep so well. But the bed was as comfortable as it was beautiful, and it was past seven when Miriam's gentle tap on her door woke her up.

To start with, she'd knock Thorne on his ear, she thought, glancing through her wardrobe hurriedly. She looked again, more slowly, hoping that by some miracle, a terrific dress she'd forgotten about would appear. It didn't.

Nearly everything she owned had been passed on to her by her sister. Becky had a whopping clothes budget and tired quickly of her purchases. She was forever mailing things to Addie, and on each of her visits, she brought something else. Although Addie wasn't a penny-pincher, she found that she couldn't in all conscience buy more outfits when her closet was already bulging with her sister's castoffs.

Since Becky's naturally light brown hair had been dyed to a startling copper, she bought muted colors—primarily browns, tans and grays, so that she "dominated" everything she wore, as she put it.

In desperation, Addie selected a beige pantsuit. At least her accessories were her own, and the orange-and-green paisley scarf added a bit of flair to the otherwise drab costume.

Her glossy brown hair, usually unmanageable in damp weather, was on its best behavior this morning. Tumbling smoothly to her shoulders, it had the unusual quality of reflecting any available light, which made it seem touched by the sun, even on drab sunless days. Though she didn't generally use eyeliner, she experimented with it now and liked the effect. She needed only a touch of coral lipstick, and she'd be on her way.

Breakfast was served in the room aptly called the breakfast room, and the buffet table held an array of food to break the will of the most determined dieter. Miriam selected French toast and chilled berries. The combination looked delicious, and Addie helped herself to the same.

Thorne arrived a few minutes early. She suspected it wasn't because he looked forward to spending the day in her company, but because he was a scheduled sort of person. Time was money. Striding through the door at ten miles an hour, he seemed to bring the brisk morning air inside with him. Had he dressed with any thought of pleasing her? It was unlikely, but he'd succeeded, anyway. He wore the same off-white windbreaker, tan slacks, a pale blue shirt, open at the collar, and a boyish smile that would have charmed her silly, if she hadn't glimpsed his other side the night before.

"Good morning, Miriam." He bent down to kiss the pale cheek the woman offered. Then he turned his eyes, shining and hard as gemstones, on Addie. "Adeline."

"Mr. Cameron—Thorne," she corrected herself before he could, and nodded her acknowledgment, though it seemed a stilted greeting, like something out of an old play.

"It's much too early in the day for anyone to be so cheerful. Settle somewhere." Miriam fluttered one hand, and Addie could tell she was attempting to disguise her pleasure at seeing him. It was likely an old game she played. "Have a cup of tea—that is, coffee. And some breakfast."

"I've already eaten," Thorne said. "Finish up now, and hurry. Time's wasting." He looked over the fare on the breakfast buffet, snatched up a plate and began to fill it with some of everything. He'd already had breakfast? Addie wondered. And now he was going to eat all that? He must do about five hundred sit-ups a day to keep such a trim stomach.

"If you two expect me to traipse all over town with you, you've got your signals crossed," Miriam said. "There's neither stick nor stone I haven't seen a hundred times. Besides, I'm just getting over a cold." To add credence to her excuse, she sniffed and cleared her throat.

Keeping her eyes averted, Addie chased the last piece of French toast around her plate. Her aunt's backing out at the last minute was a none-too-subtle way of providing the "young people" with hours alone together. She knew it and so did Thorne.

"I'd rather spend a quiet day here myself, Miriam," Addie tried again. "The sights of the city can wait."

No one spoke for a moment. Although she wasn't looking directly at Thorne, he was in her peripheral vision. He'd put down his fork and was smoothing a tanned squarish hand along a wrinkled place in the linen tablecloth. "Do either of you young ladies realize how much juggling I had to do to arrange these days off?"

These days? Plural? Apparently he was offering a package deal. "I'm sorry." Addie forced her golden eyes to his steely ones. The impact almost sent her toppling. His anger was clear. How could Miriam miss it?

"Sorry doesn't cut it." His voice held an unmistakable edge.

What was his problem? She'd let him off the hook.

"You see," she went on, as if she hadn't noticed his reaction, "I'm planning to copy all of Miriam's family photographs. I have a special camera that can do it perfectly without the use of a flash if the light is right. It was shamefully expensive, but worth every penny. I didn't want one of those drop-in, click-click, snap-snap affairs. Not when—"

She broke off at once when she realized she'd been jabbering, saying things she wouldn't have said if Thorne hadn't subjected her to that stare of his. By going on about the price of the camera, she'd only reinforced his belief that she was bent on playing the "poor little working girl" for Miriam's benefit.

"Of course you're going," Miriam said, with a touch of petulance. "Why should you miss all the excitement just because I'm too tired to go gallivanting?"

"Tired?" Thorne laughed. "Don't let her fool you, Adeline. The truth is, she's a soap-opera addict and is afraid if she's gone for the day, she won't find out who did what to whom."

Miriam feigned surprise. "However did you guess?"

"Part of my job is knowing what makes people tick." He tapped a finger against his forehead and looked at Addie again. "You, for example, are stalling for time, hoping I'll go away. You don't know me very well."

"It makes no sense for me to usurp your day," she insisted. It was one thing to put up with him when Miriam was present to keep him on his best behavior. It was quite another to have him all to herself. "A car is an inconvenience here, from what I've heard. The subway takes a person anywhere in no time, and I'll certainly be able to find the Freedom Trail. I'll just follow it from one historical site to the next. That way I'll get to see everything from Paul Revere's house to Copp's Hill Burying Ground.''

"But did you know that Isaiah and Ezekiel Rutherford are buried at Copp's Hill?'' Miriam asked.

"No, I didn't.''

"There you go. Thorne will be able to lead you right to their graves.''

"You can take pictures of their markers with that magnificent camera,'' he added with exaggerated solemnity. He pushed back his chair. "Are you ready to go?''

"Almost.'' Resigned to the inevitable, Addie set her napkin beside her plate. "I'd like to call home first if it's all right.''

"Certainly, dear,'' Miriam answered. "That'll give Thorne time to finish his coffee. And I want a few words with him, anyway.''

During Addie's conversation with her grandfather the night before, he'd told her he would receive word on the new loan this morning. He always got up early, and she knew he'd be sitting at the breakfast table alone now, drinking too much coffee as he waited and stewed. A word or two of encouragement couldn't hurt, and might help.

As she'd anticipated, he pooh-poohed her concern. Worry? Not him. If the bank didn't come through, he had a few other irons in the fire. She was to concentrate on why she was in Boston and think no more about the business.

"What's on the agenda for today?'' he asked.

"The Freedom Trail,'' she said, trying to sound cheery.

"What about all those pictures you're supposed to get for the family album?''

"I'll get them.''

"Don't be too sure. Some folks are mighty funny about photographs. They don't even like other folks touching 'em."

"Don't worry," Addie assured him. "Miriam trusts me implicitly. I'll get everything I came for, and much, much more."

Thorne had come in so quietly that she felt his presence before she heard him. He was at her elbow, tapping impatient fingers against his thigh as he waited.

"Goodbye, little girl," Barney said. "Kiss Cousin Miriam for me."

"I will. I love you."

"Nothing like confidence," Thorne said, helping her with her jacket.

"Pardon?" The calculating look in his eyes rankled her, and she was in no mood to humor him.

Poor Barney. Maybe she should forget all about Boston and fly home. Her place was with him.

Or would he consider her return to his side an insult?

"I heard you telling your grandfather you planned to get everything you came for and much, much more."

She wriggled out of his grasp. "Eavesdropping on a private conversation? Now why doesn't that surprise me?"

"If what you had to say was private, I would have thought you'd use one of the extensions."

She sighed and spoke with exaggerated patience. "When I said I'd get everything I came for, I was referring to family photographs. It's important to him that I get as many as— Oh, forget it." Why give credence to his insult by dwelling on it? She burst ahead of him to the door. "If you're so eager to go, let's go."

"Goodbye, darlings." Miriam emerged from the breakfast room and kissed Addie on one cheek, then the other. "If you return in time, Thorne has promised to take us out to see something of Boston nightlife. Won't that be fun?"

Nightlife. So that was why she'd wanted to speak with Thorne alone. She wanted to twist his arm a bit more. Addie had a difficult time containing a groan of frustration.

Fun? That wasn't the word Addie would have used for it at all.

"Do your friends call you Adeline?" he asked when they were on their way.

"Why shouldn't they?"

"It doesn't suit you."

"Because I have freckles?"

"Have you?" He didn't turn toward her. "I didn't notice. No, it's the way you respond to the name. As if it takes you a moment to realize you're the one being addressed."

"Most people call me Addie," she said, deciding that such perception should be rewarded with truth.

He nodded, satisfied. They would take the northern loop of the Freedom Trail, he told her. It would be best to get an overview of the city first, then decide what they would revisit for closer inspection later.

It was a good plan, and one she'd already worked out for herself. The path they walked was so rich in history, her antagonism toward the man beside her faded, and before long, she felt transported to another time.

When they arrived at the cemetery, he opened the black iron gate to allow them entrance. Solemnly they moved among the leaning and weathered gravestones until they came to the plots of Isaiah and Ezekiel Rutherford.

She set her camera stops with meticulous care, circling the spot, watching the shifting shadows to capture the best effect, even dropping to one knee, as she took shot after shot.

Thorne's laugh distracted her. "What?" she asked, laughing, too.

"If you could see your face."

"Is it dirty?" She lifted a hand to her cheek. "What's wrong with it?"

"Absolutely nothing. It's very beautiful. You're... glowing." His smile was gone now and an intense expression shadowed his eyes.

Still holding the camera poised for a shot, she found herself staring at him. If a man could be described as beautiful, Thorne was that man. Spears of sunlight, appearing and disappearing as the breeze ruffled the surrounding trees, emphasized his strong bone structure and dramatic features.

"Thank you," she said, remembering how often she'd heard that the best way to answer a compliment, whether sincere or not, was polite acceptance. "I still want to know what made you laugh."

"You. Thrilling over the graves of men who've been dead for two hundred years."

"It probably sounds foolish to you," she conceded.

"It sounds like an obsession. I wonder. Is there a living breathing man who can put the same fire in your eyes?"

That was the kind of question Frank might have asked. Coming from Thorne, it set her off balance. "I used to feel just like you do," she said, brushing over his question to pick up the thread of what they'd been discussing. "As I said, I began digging into the past to please Barney. Family is everything to him."

"Barney. Your grandfather."

"Yes. And before I realized what was happening, I was caught up in it. I began to feel like Sherlock Holmes. Hot on the trail of an important discovery."

She hadn't succeeded in distracting him from what he wanted to know. She could tell he was only half listening, puzzling over her words. What sort of women was he used to? Didn't they have consuming interests or hobbies? Or once Thorne came into their lives, did *he* become that interest? She could see how that might happen.

Until then, they'd had the cemetery all to themselves. Now an elderly woman was coming up the path, carrying pink roses and a jar filled with water. Smiling at Thorne and Addie as if the three shared a common mission, she picked her way through the rows. When she found the marker she wanted, she knelt and began arranging her flowers.

"Could we...?" Addie began, thinking of Isaiah and Ezekiel.

Thorne shrugged. "Why not? Allow me." He retreated, then came back a few minutes later with a mixed bouquet he'd bought from a vendor outside the gates. "Only one left. They'll have to share."

"I don't think they'll mind. Thank you."

Neither of them spoke as she plucked out the unwanted grasses and divided the bouquet. "There now."

The breezes were stronger than they had been, and cooler. As Thorne helped her to her feet, a lock of toffee-brown hair blew across her eyes. "It's as soft and fine as a child's," he observed, reaching out and brushing it back.

"I should probably wear it in a braid." Fighting against the inner flutter his touch had caused, she brought a nervous hand to her forehead. "To keep it out of my face and let me see where I'm going when the wind blows."

"Flying about, it gives you the look of a woodland creature."

What kind of creature? she questioned silently. Was that a compliment or an insult? When she'd dressed that morning she'd intended to anchor her hair with a clip. Now she wished she had.

What was he thinking? There was something in his face she hadn't seen before. More important, there was something going on inside her she'd never felt before. This man, in the few short hours they'd spent together, had managed to evoke the entire range of her emotions. But the one she was feeling now was the most unwelcome.

She didn't want to like him too much. She'd only be here for two weeks. After that, she might never see him again. It was a good thing, too, given his opinion of her—which she felt sure he'd only put on hold in the interests of congenial sight-seeing.

"It *can* be uncomfortable at times," she said, reaching somewhat desperately for a safer subject.

"Your hair?" His gaze settled on her lips, and she steeled herself for her overreaction.

"No. Doing research. It can be uncomfortable. It's cold in the microfilm room and my feet are usually freezing no matter how warmly I dress. My vision blurs from trying to decipher the faded handwriting on old documents. I get motion sickness from flipping the pages, and my back begins to ache."

"That's your idea of fun?"

"Not exactly. But then I come across a will, a deed, a passenger list—something that points me in the right direction—and all the discomfort is worth it. You'd be surprised at the dignified people who let out shrieks of joy when they locate what they've been looking for. It's a thrill I can't explain."

"A thrill?" One eyebrow quirked.

"There are all sorts of thrills," she told him, then wished she hadn't when he looked amused.

"Your eyes are orange," he said. "No. Gold. I've never seen any quite like them."

"They're brown." She shrugged, trying to appear offhand. "Plain everyday brown."

"I can see them. You can't."

Still studying her, he put his hands on her shoulders, and she emitted a small startled cry. Would he kiss her here? Now? She steadied herself, fearing that the force of it might make her light-headed. But a kiss wasn't what he had in mind.

"Stand here," he said, maneuvering her to a place between Ezekiel and Isaiah. "I'll get a shot of you. Who knows? We might get one of those spirit photographs I've read about. One of the old boys might put in an appearance and make your day."

Feeling foolish, she managed a weak smile for the camera. Had Thorne guessed that she'd anticipated a kiss? Had he made the swift move toward her purposely, wanting her to think exactly what she'd thought?

Of course not. He hadn't brought her here to play games. He hadn't even brought her here for his own pleasure. She'd been wished on him, and she'd better start remembering that, in case she found herself looking too deeply into those captivating blue eyes.

The Public Gardens were alive with early spring colors—cherry blossoms and masses of tulips—calling for more photographs. Then they moved to the iron bridge over the lagoon and watched the swan boats. The spot was so pleasant, so peaceful, Addie hoped they might linger.

"They build their freeways and demolish their historical buildings to make room for glass monstrosities, but the old city shines through it all." He leaned forward, with his elbows on the rail. "A ghost that refuses to be evicted. It remains what it was, and progress be damned."

"It must be glorious in the winter with skaters on the ice and the trees heavy with snow." She turned toward him.

He shivered. "Beautiful and cold. Think a California girl could take it?"

"We get snow in the mountains."

"You get snow. But you don't know what winter is until you've experienced a New England winter."

"I'll take your word for it." Familiar now with the change in his facial expression that signaled his desire to leave, Addie touched his sleeve. "No more today."

"Had enough?" His eyes were a clear blue in the pale afternoon light. The wind had ruffled his hair. A lock of it fell across his forehead, which made her want to smooth it back, as he had done with hers. "No more history?"

"It's been wonderful. But my feet are throbbing."

He lifted a hand to return the wave of a little girl on one of the boats. "I shouldn't admit this, but I've only been braving it out, wanting you to holler uncle."

"Really?" His admission warmed her.

"Really. You want to start home?"

"Yes. No. That is, if you don't mind, I'd like to do a little shopping first." It wasn't something she would have mentioned to the impatient Thorne Cameron he'd been when they set off. The new man he'd become would understand.

His eyes crinkled boyishly when he smiled.

"It isn't what you think," she protested, not wanting him to assume, as many men did, that women thought only of spending money. "I just want to pick up a couple of things...."

He rotated his wrist to look at his watch. "You have an hour, tops. Miriam will get nervous about dinner reservations if we aren't back."

"An hour will be more than enough."

It wasn't. There was too much to see. At the first store she fell in love with a green sweater. At the second, it was a pair of shoes that were mostly straps, and at a third, it was an oversize scarf in shades of pink that would have been lovely on Miriam. Everything was entirely too expensive, however, and when her time was up, she'd bought only a few postcards and a jigsaw puzzle for Barney. A map of Massachusetts.

Despite their poor start, Thorne had been a perfect partner for her introduction to Boston. He hadn't grumbled at her indecision or even glanced at a clock to remind her of her deadline. Maybe he'd even revised his opinion of her. When he offered his arm on the way to the car, she took it, enjoying the feeling of being close to him.

The next chance she had to shop, she'd buy something for him as a thank-you and to show him there were no hard feelings for the way things had begun between them. A book, or possibly a record. During the course of the day's meanderings, she'd learned he was an aficionado of big-band music, Glen Miller in particular.

"Oh, look!" She tugged at his arm. Among the rings and wristwatches in a jewelry store display window lay a shimmering emerald necklace in an old-fashioned setting. "Isn't it exquisite?"

He whistled. "Emeralds. You're a girl of simple tastes."

"My grandmother, Barney's wife, had two pieces of heirloom jewelry. A diamond ring, she left to my sister, Becky, and a necklace very much like that one, she left to me."

"Very nice."

"I never had the chance to wear it. My sister borrowed it for a special evening, and the clasp broke. She took it with her, promising to have it fixed. Then she phoned to say she preferred the necklace to the ring, anyway. Would I be willing to trade? We argued back and forth about it. Then a couple of weeks ago she had a burglary. Somehow the thief or thieves overlooked her diamond. But they made off with my necklace, a portable TV and an electric toothbrush."

"That's too bad."

She sighed, unable to take her eyes off the necklace. "It reminds me so much of Gram. I wish I could afford to buy it."

"For the sentiment."

"Yes. Sometimes she allowed me to wear it, when I was little and . . ." Addie looked up at him, at the window and back again, wondering if she'd really heard something insinuating in his voice. "And played dress-up at her house."

"Save your sad little tale for Miriam," he said abruptly, steering her away. "It's wasted on me."

"What tale?"

"It got me right here." He thumped a fist against his chest. "But it's unnecessary. Miriam's so taken with you, she'd delight in throwing away money on expensive little baubles you might fancy. Yes, I have no doubt you'll get 'everything you came for and much, much more.'"

She yanked her arm away. "That isn't funny."

"You're right. It isn't." He looked down at her through narrowed eyes.

"You're halfway serious, aren't you? You still see me as grasping and mercenary."

"Does it matter how I see you?"

"No, it doesn't," she agreed, walking faster.

Unbelievably, during the ride home, he kept up his lively patter, pointing out houses where famous people had once lived, talking about the current exhibits at the museum, and holding forth on his own habit of jogging along the river early in the morning or in the evenings after work. It was therapy for him.

Good. He needed all the therapy he could get.

How could he not realize that she was hurt and angry? If he was too stone-headed to see the insult in his humor, he should have been able to tell from her silence as they rode back to Miriam's house that she'd rather not hear his voice. But no, he kept talking.

"Don't you get out here, too?" she asked when they arrived, and he only sat, watching her.

"Yes. But I pull around in back and park in the garage."

"Don't bother walking me to the door, then," she said archly. "You can sit here and watch, in case anyone pounces on me from the bushes."

"Pity the poor unsuspecting wretch who tangles with you tonight."

"You're right about that," she agreed, fastening him with a scowl she hoped would mirror all the contempt she felt. "I've never had anyone go out of his way to offend me before."

His lips curved in disdain. "I'm sure you haven't. You have such a sweet innocent face, no one thinks to look any closer."

"Goodbye, Thorne. And thank you—I suppose." Not trusting herself to say more, she reached for the door handle.

"Wait." He clamped a hand over hers. "Tell Miriam I'll be there around eight. If that doesn't work with her dinner plans, she can give me a call."

Dinner. She'd almost forgotten they'd be seeing each other again in a couple of hours.

Pointedly, she looked first at the hand that restrained her, then into Thorne's eyes, now darkly brooding. If he was contemplating some further hurt, she had no intention of remaining to accept it. "Is there anything else?"

"As a matter of fact, yes." His voice was sandpapery, and his face, smoothly shaven that morning, was now shadowed with beard, which didn't at all detract from his sensual appearance. Coupled with the slightly disheveled inky-black hair, it gave him the heroic look of a storybook prince.

"Well?"

"One more thing." Making a sound low in his throat, he dropped his hand. Then he half-dragged, half-lifted her toward him.

Never before had she felt fragile or helpless. Now she felt both, as he forced her into his arms, allowing his mouth full access to hers. It was a brief but stunning kiss, one that possessed her, leaving her unable to speak or move. When he let her go, she wasn't aware of it immediately, and only lay in his arms.

Little by little, her senses returned, and she twisted away from him, working hard to resume her normal breathing pattern.

"That was contemptible," she managed huskily. "And predictable."

"Would you have kissed me willingly?"

"Can you ask that with a straight face? A kiss is a token of affection. Affection is the last thing I feel for you."

"There you have it." He slapped the steering wheel lightly. "It had to be done."

She stared at him. "*Had* to be done?"

"Miriam would have been disappointed if you'd come home with lipstick intact."

Gritting her teeth in frustration, she brought her fingers to her lips, now beginning to burn. "How thoughtful you are! Always willing to make sacrifices to please other people."

"I do what I can." He tried to look modest.

She got out and stood with a hand on the car door, wanting to be sure she was steady on her feet. "Miriam!" she threw at him with a toss of her head. "Don't pretend you gave in to your animal instincts just for her."

"Very well, I won't." His smile was more maddening than his scowl. "As long as you don't pretend you didn't want it, too."

"I—I—" The denial was there, waiting to be uttered, but she wasn't able to get it past her lips. "You're despicable."

"And you're repeating yourself." He turned the key in the ignition as she ran up the steps. "Remember. Eight o'clock. And be ready. I'm not very good at waiting."

CHAPTER FOUR

"WHAT DO YOU HAVE against the Grenvilles?" Miriam was in the sitting room, talking with someone. She peered over the reading glasses perched on the end of her nose and held out a welcoming arm to Addie. "You're back. Good."

"You can't have the Grenvilles if you're having the Montgomerys," a masculine voice explained.

"Why on earth can't I?"

"The Montgomery boy jilted the Grenville girl last autumn. Putting the two couples at the same table might be interesting, but it wouldn't do much for congenial conversation." A young man with sun-streaked dark blond hair rose from a wing chair, the back of which faced the door so that Addie hadn't been able to see him at first. He was holding a book with a picture of a screaming woman on the cover. One finger was stuck between the pages to mark his place. He had coffee-brown eyes, a straight blunt nose and a crushing hand-shake.

"Sweet Adeline," he crooned appreciatively before Miriam had a chance to introduce them.

"So original," she purred. "I'll bet no one has sung her that one since the little boy in the desk behind her dunked her ponytail in the inkwell. Adeline, this is my nephew, Kevin Roper."

"I'm happy to meet you, Kevin," Addie said, carefully recovering her fingers from his grasp.

"Kevin had pressing business in Albany, but he flew back just to meet his newfound cousin." She turned one of her brightest smiles on her nephew. "So, is she worth the trip?"

"Worth even the cardboard steak they served me on the plane," he pronounced.

"You used the flight time to improve your mind, I see." She cast a disapproving look at the lurid cover of his book, before turning her attention back to Addie. "I don't know if you've gathered from our conversation that I'm planning a party in your honor."

"You mustn't," Addie protested, hoping her voice didn't betray the unhappiness she felt after her degrading exchange with Thorne. "I'd rather you didn't make any fuss over me."

Miriam looked hurt. "But I'm proud of you, darling. How else can I introduce you to all my friends in the short time you'll be here? Please don't deny me this one pleasure."

Addie glanced from Miriam to Kevin and then to Miriam again. "I won't," she said, recognizing defeat. "If you're sure it isn't too much trouble."

"It's a delight," the woman said. "Now we'd better get dressed for our gala evening. What time will Thorne be here?"

"Eight o'clock."

"Good." Miriam started to leave, then turned back. "Kevin, why don't you come along? It would be good if you and Thorne saw each other socially now and then. It might help you work through your differences."

"I think not." Kevin shook his head. "Anyway, after the tangle at the airport, I want to relax."

He followed Addie into the entrance hall as Miriam swept up the stairs. "Cameron is showing you the sights, is he? Too bad."

"Why do you say that?"

"No doubt you've seen the Old North Church and the Boston Common."

"Among other things."

"I can show you parts of the city not shown in guidebooks." He dropped his voice to a theatrical whisper and waggled his shaggy brows for emphasis.

"For instance?"

"Oh, the spot where there was a murder most foul, one dark night in 1849, for example. Or, if you prefer going farther afield, Fall River. Lizzie Borden's stomping ground."

"As in 'Lizzie Borden took an ax'? No, thank you." Addie held up one hand as if to push away the picture. "I'll stick to the more usual tourist sights."

"More thrills in my guidebook."

"I don't doubt it." She grinned at him. "But I'm a simple girl with simple tastes."

He chewed on his lower lip. "Not so simple, I'm thinking. Not so simple at all."

"I'd better go upstairs and change now," she said. If she gave her hair a merciless brushing and indulged in a perfumed soak, she might feel better about what had happened between her and Thorne, though she doubted it. "Will I see you later?"

"My room is only a few doors from yours. Drop in anytime." His hand closed over hers where it rested on the banister, but his touch was casual, not provocative. "Maybe you'll agree to take a stroll with me tomorrow, or the next day. You haven't seen Boston until you've done a turn on Beacon Hill."

"Maybe," she replied, her voice lacking conviction. "It depends on what Miriam has in mind."

"Are you sure you're not just afraid to go with me?"

She smiled quizzically. "Why should I be?"

"Oh, my taste in literature." He gestured at his book.

"Not at all. I enjoy mysteries, too."

"I'm said to be a very nice fellow. Likable, sweet, considerate, polite..."

"And humble?"

"That, too. Easily crushed by rejection."

"I can see that."

You're a nice man, Kevin Roper, she wanted to tell him. *But it's a bad time for me.* She wasn't up to the flirtatious banter people indulge in when they've just met and are attracted to each other.

"So can I chalk that up as a definite maybe?" he persisted.

She nodded. "You can."

Now why had she said that? she wondered later, as she was standing in front of her closet, trying to decide what to wear. She had no intention of taking up with Miriam's nephew, no matter how nice he was. Thorne would only see their friendship as another sign that Addie was trying to ingratiate herself with the family.

"Adeline?" Miriam tapped on the door and came in, without waiting for an answer. "I forgot to ask. Did you bring an evening dress?"

"Yes, I did."

"Good. I'll look in later. Do your hair in an upsweep, won't you, darling?" The woman touched her fingers to Addie's forehead. "With a fringe of curls here and over each ear. It'd be so much more romantic-looking, don't you think?"

Romantic, Addie thought ruefully, dressed now, and studying her reflection in the mirror. Her evening gown was an innocuous ivory-beige crepe. Since Becky had sent it to her only last week, she hadn't had occasion to wear it before. But as the sisters wore approximately the same size, she'd known it would fit fairly well.

With her hair swept into a rich caramel-colored riot of curls atop her head, the low-cut neckline exposed far too much creamy skin. The effect wasn't at all what she wanted.

"If only my neck weren't so long." She turned from one side to the other, frowning at her mirror image, not realizing she said the words aloud or that Miriam had appeared in the doorway.

"In my day, a long graceful neck was desirable," the woman assured her. "It was a mark of beauty."

"There's long, and then there's long." Addie drew the words out comically. "Do I have time to change?" Into what? Her sweater dress? No, of course not. Her gray silk shirtwaist? Possibly.

"You'll do no such thing. The neckline simply needs something."

"Yes. A muffler."

Miriam tittered girlishly. "I know just the thing. Let me show you." She gestured for Addie to follow her.

Shyly, like a child who had a secret she couldn't keep to herself any longer, the woman opened the louvered doors of the cherrywood dresser in her own bedroom, revealing a shallow drawer that held an array of old-fashioned earrings and brooches, each in its own satin nest.

She reached underneath, and clucked her tongue impatiently. "Help me, won't you, dear? I don't want to muss my hair putting on my glasses. There's a metal ring at the back. Turn it clockwise.''

Curious, Addie slid her fingers along the lower edge of the drawer. There was a clicking sound, indicating that a catch had been released, and at Miriam's direction she slid the drawer out completely and set it on the bed.

Glancing at Addie again with mischief twinkling in her eyes, the older woman took a jewel box from the hidden compartment. "It needs this," she said, handing it to Addie.

Resting inside the box on a bed of gray velvet was a brilliant sapphire, surrounded by diamonds, on a delicate gold chain.

Addie gasped. "I've never seen anything so exquisite," she said, when she found her voice. "But...oh, I do hope you don't expect me to wear it. It might snag on something and slip off. I appreciate the thought, but I couldn't possibly..."

"You can and you will." Miriam was already fastening the clasp. "Why should it lie in a box in a musty drawer when the two of you complement each other so splendidly?" Beaming, she stepped back to admire the effect. "You look like a princess preparing to meet her prince."

"I don't know what to say." Gingerly, Addie touched the necklace, sliding her fingers under it to feel its weight. The dazzling beauty of the blue stone had transformed the dress—had transformed *her* into someone she hardly recognized. Her eyes were truly golden, as Thorne had said they were, and the curve of her neck seemed exactly right now.

"Don't say anything," Miriam insisted, taking Addie's arm to lead her toward the stairs. "Let's not spoil our evening with petty bickering."

Petty bickering. Addie had to smile at the choice of words. She was learning something about the older woman. Gentle as she might be, delicate-seeming and fragile, she had a will of iron and was clearly used to getting her own way.

And why not? Her kindness made her well-deserving. Addie would just have to be careful. She was so acutely aware of the necklace, anyway, she'd certainly notice if it slipped from her neck.

Thorne had arrived. He was in the entrance hall with Kevin. Though their voices were low, it was obvious they'd had a disagreement. Thorne, apparently, was unhappy about the other man's turning his out-of-town business over to someone else.

"Your place is at that conference table," he growled.

"My place is any damn place I decide to make it," Kevin shot back.

Addie hesitated at the top of the stairs, wanting for Miriam's sake, to wait until the less-than-friendly exchange was over before starting down. So, she wasn't the only one who'd earned Thorne's disapproval. The realization made her like Kevin even more. At least they had something in common.

Thorne's eyes glimmered with the memory of their last meeting as he caught sight of her. Surprisingly, they held a caress rather than the taunt she'd expected. His slow appreciative smile reminded her of how the heated pressure of his mouth had felt on hers. She had to take the stairs carefully to keep from tumbling down.

Expectancy of the moment had whirled her into such a state of sensitivity that when he grasped her hand in greeting, she almost flowed into his arms.

"Isn't my girl the picture of loveliness tonight?" Miriam stood on tiptoe to collect Thorne's kiss, then slid an arm around him.

Kevin's answer was an appreciative whistle.

"She is that," Thorne agreed. He dipped his head slightly, using the question as an excuse for a closer appraisal.

"Would it be unforgivably conceited of me to say that she reminds me of myself at her age?" Miriam went on. "I noticed the resemblance at the airport. It struck me speechless."

"That's a wonderful compliment," Addie said gently, noting the quaver in the older woman's voice.

"I don't give compliments. Judge for yourself." Miriam gestured toward a sepia-toned photograph of a younger Miriam with upswept hair and a fringe of bangs across her forehead.

There was a surface resemblance, Addie conceded, though it wasn't nearly as strong as Miriam chose to believe. But it wasn't the face in the photograph that made her look closer. When she did, she gasped.

The older woman smiled at her reaction. "Yes. You're wearing the same necklace. Dear George gave it to me as a wedding gift, and I adored it. It made me feel beautiful."

"As if you needed any artificial adornment for that, Auntie," Kevin said gallantly.

Addie forced her eyes from the photograph to her own image in the gold-veined mirror. Was this why Miriam wanted her hair in an upsweep? The weight of the sapphire at the base of her throat seemed tenfold now.

"Are you sure you want me to wear it?" she asked. "This necklace is so valuable..."

Valuable wasn't the word she'd been searching for. It had a calculating mercenary sound, and the worth of the stone was measured by so much more.

"Valuable." Miriam jumped on it. "Poof. Don't be tiresome. You're family now. George would want it worn."

"Then *you* should wear it."

"My skin tone has changed. I look ghastly in blue these days. I know it's not the same as your grandmother's necklace, the one that was stolen from you. But to be frank, I believe the sapphire is more becoming to you than an emerald would be." Miriam went on at great length, telling Thorne about Addie's grandmother's necklace and the burglar who made off with it.

He didn't mention that he already knew the story, and his eyes, every bit as hard as the blue stone Addie wore, were fixed accusingly on her face. The smile that curved his lips was a forced unpleasant one.

He actually saw Miriam's loan of the necklace as a result of Addie's hints about her feelings of loss when the emerald was stolen. The realization threatened to smother her. Should she explain to him about the newsy letters she'd written, relating the most insignificant and routine parts of her daily life? Should she tell him again that she'd sent those letters when she had no idea that Miriam would be in a financial position to present her with gifts of any kind?

No. Why should she? Moments before, he'd been devouring her with his eyes. Now he was looking as if he'd stepped down from Mount Olympus to judge her. How dared he?

If his attitude said anything about what she might expect from the rest of Miriam's supposedly fun-filled evening, she wasn't sure she was up to it. As she allowed herself to be helped into the waiting car, her thoughts were grim.

The first club they visited had a prohibition-era atmosphere. The next was a lively disco frequented by the college crowd. But it was easy to see that Thorne had saved his favorite for last.

A glass elevator that afforded a superlative view of the city took them to a covered rooftop garden, where the orchestra, with its big-band sound, might have been transported from the forties. It even had a vocalist with old-fashioned hair ribbons and pompadour, and a quartet of swing-era "doo-ah" singers. Best of all were the slow romantic ballads, their meaningful lyrics and mellow sounds crying out for a special dancing partner.

If she hadn't known better, she wouldn't have guessed anything was wrong. Thorne was pleasant and attentive. Even when they danced, he made no reference to her supposed cupidity.

He asked politely how her family research was going. She told him of her plans to go to the public library. She'd heard they had an extensive genealogical collection. He suggested trying the facilities at Harvard.

"I'll take you," he offered, as they moved around the crowded dance floor to the strains of "Always." "I have friends in the research library who might be able to help."

"No, thank you," she said quickly, echoing his oh-so-polite tone. "Miriam's offered me the use of her car, and my background in medical records should open a few doors if I decide to try the university." In other words, she wanted nothing more from him.

The hand at her back shifted. "Miriam doesn't want you wandering around a strange city by yourself."

"I'll be fine."

"I know you will." One steely blue eye narrowed almost imperceptibly. "I'll be with you."

Think again, Mr. Cameron, she almost threw at him, wearying of the drawing-room courtesy. "I'd rather not structure my time yet. I might even decide to stay home with Miriam."

"Stay home with Miriam," he repeated, a small play of his handsome features making the remark insinuating.

"Afraid I'll convince her to sign her property over to me?" she asked, compelled by the need to clear the air.

"Why should I worry about that? Only because you've played on Miriam's desire to recapture the past by wearing your hair exactly as she did when she was young? Because you've been here only twenty-four hours, and she's already lent you one of her most precious possessions, the necklace George gave her when they were married?"

"I didn't want to spoil the evening with an argument. I simply thought my wearing it would make her happy..." Her voice trailed off. He clearly didn't believe her, and the suspicion in his eyes made her feel lost and empty. Talking about this further was pointless. "May we go back and sit down?" she asked abruptly.

"When the music stops."

"Now."

"Miriam is watching." Any attempt to escape his grasp would have been futile, or at the very least, would have caused a scene. His hold was firm. She could feel each of his fingers searing the skin at the small of her back.

"You've been insufferable tonight."

"What you find insufferable is that your charms haven't toppled me." One eyebrow peaked and he nearly smiled. "I'll admit it was close, though."

She looked toward their table. Miriam was watching them as intently as a stage mother might watch her darlings perform. How little she guessed of what was truly going on.

At last the song was over. The orchestra began to play "Tuxedo Junction" and Thorne courteously guided Addie back to the table.

"It's as if the two of you have danced together hundreds of times," Miriam cooed. "Such a pleasure to watch you."

Addie swallowed hard. Not as adept as her partner at playacting, she was grateful that the lights were dim enough to disguise her true feelings.

Battling inside herself, she found very little to say for the rest of the evening. It didn't matter. Miriam chattered as she usually did when she was having a good time, and Thorne inserted humorous courtroom tales into the remaining conversational gaps. The tension took its toll on Addie, however, and by the time they got home, she was emotionally exhausted.

Predictably, Miriam insisted that Thorne come in for a nightcap. There were some papers she'd found among her late husband's things. She wanted him to look them over and see if they were the ones he'd been trying to locate. George Mandeville had been a shrewd businessman, but he'd been less than methodical about keeping his records in one place, where they'd be readily accessible.

"There are other things at the farm," she said. "Several boxes tied up with string and stacked on a closet shelf. If what I have here isn't what you need, we can drive to Belton tomorrow, the three of us, and see about them."

"Since Roper saw fit to drop the Albany business in someone else's lap and fly home, he doesn't have anything to do. Why don't you give him the keys to the place?" Thorne suggested. "He could make the drive and save you a trip."

"I don't want to be saved the trip, dear one. It would be a nice outing for Adeline." She smiled at Addie. "I have some photographs tucked away there, too. I know she'd like to see them. Besides, you really need to look at those papers yourself. Why should Kevin drag them all the way back to the city if they aren't what you need?"

"Very well." Thorne hesitated just long enough to let Addie know he wasn't enthusiastic about the plans. "If you're sure you want to go."

"I'm sure." Miriam squeezed his arm. "It'll be good for you to get away, too. You work much too hard."

No sooner were they in the house and settled than, also predictably, Miriam developed a "splitting" headache. "I'll have a cup of cocoa in my room and go to bed," she announced, pressing her fingers to the bridge of her nose. "Adeline, come upstairs with me. I'll give you the papers I have, then the two of you can finish your drinks and have a nice chat. I don't want to spoil your evening."

The ploy to give them time alone was so obvious, Addie felt more than a little embarrassed when she returned with the manila envelope her aunt had given her.

"These are letters," she said, "referring to property Mr. Mandeville wanted to acquire in . . . I don't know." She fluttered one hand. "It's all in there."

"Mmm." Absently, he undid the clasp and pulled out the contents, only to thumb through them before putting them back again. "I'll go over these later."

Was he feeling discomfort, too? Surprisingly, she thought he was. His thoughts, like hers, seemed to be far away from the bitter words they had flung at each other earlier. Nor did he seem to be thinking about the missing property papers and the drive they would reluctantly be taking the next morning.

During the day and early evening, members of the household staff were usually about—dusting, polishing, answering the telephone or merely standing by—but they had evidently all retired tonight. The silence was disconcerting. The room itself seemed transformed. Miriam had clicked off the overhead lights in the hall as she withdrew, leaving a soft peach glow from the fan-shaped wall lamps. She might have clicked off the antagonism between Addie and Thorne, as well, from the warmth that now embraced them in the silence of the evening.

"I'll say good-night then." Addie tried to break the spell, and she moved into the hallway. He followed right behind.

"You do resemble her, you know," he said.

"I don't see it." They both looked at the old photograph of Miriam again, though it was too faded for close inspection in the dimly lit foyer.

"She was a beautiful young woman."

Deciding not to accept the compliment paid to Miriam as her own, she took a step toward the door. "Thank you for a very special evening."

Thorne didn't take the hint. "It was a photograph that brought George and Miriam together, did she tell you?"

"No, she didn't." The words ended in a whisper.

They were standing side by side now, so close that when he gestured, their arms brushed the way they had during the ride from the airport. As before, she was strongly aware of the contact. Her stomach muscles tightened, and her heart began a frenzied uneven beat.

"Trying to scrape together enough to keep his business afloat, George worked nights at a studio that took pictures for many of the high-school yearbooks," Thorne went on. "When he saw Miriam's photograph, he couldn't take his eyes off it. He managed to get her address from the records and carried it around for weeks before he had the nerve to approach her. According to George, he was so much in love with her by then, he proposed marriage an hour after they met."

"He must have been a romantic." Growing more uneasy about her nearness to Thorne with every passing second, Addie concentrated on the photograph, trying to think of something frivolous to say that would put things in perspective and allow her to move away gracefully.

"Hey." Thorne tapped a finger under her chin and raised her face for closer inspection. "Are those tears in your eyes?"

"It was a touching story," she said.

"George said that what struck him when they met was that the picture hadn't done Miriam justice. It didn't capture the delicate arch of her brow. The flawlessness of her skin, barely touched with rose. The golden lights of her hair..."

As he spoke, his finger still at her chin, his eyes on Addie now, not Miriam, she detected a change in his breathing. At the same moment, she became acutely aware of her own. "George Mandeville said those things?"

His lips hinted at a smile. "He might have."

His hand moved along her cheekbone to a place below her ear. There his fingers stayed, making her devastatingly conscious of a throbbing in that very spot. She cast a desperate look at the staircase, hoping Miriam, Teresa, the butler—someone—would appear and save her from what now seemed inevitable.

Would it help to think of something unpleasant? Her worries about Barney? Or Thorne's suspicions? Not much. Her powers of concentration were rapidly evaporating.

Letting the envelope drop onto the hall table, Thorne slid an arm around her. "I want to kiss you," he said.

"You needn't." She drew back with what remained of her strength. "Miriam isn't watching."

"I'm not thinking of Miriam."

"You're all mixed up, Mr. Cameron. One minute you want to throttle me, and the next . . ."

"The next . . ."

His other hand was at her back now, the way it had been on the dance floor. Though they stood motionless, the turmoil inside her made her feel the rhythm of the dance again, a wild pagan rhythm that, if allowed to run its course, would build in tempo until her unwilling limbs moved independently of her conscious thought.

"Addie." His eyes were smoky gray in the half-light. His lips were only a breath away. Before she could decide if she was even capable of resistance, he assaulted her unready mouth with a brief searing kiss. It saturated her senses with the flavor and scent of him, yet left her wanting more.

For mere seconds, he drew back, confusion mirrored in his eyes, before he kissed her again. This time the passion that had been smoldering almost from their first meeting erupted and cascaded through her. Her lips parted, offering a challenge he accepted without hesitation.

A door closed somewhere. A voice came from far off, one of the servants roused by Miriam's arrival. With aching slowness their lips separated. Her breath was ragged as she crushed her cheek against the roughness of his jacket.

"I shouldn't have done that," he muttered, sounding almost angry. "Under the circumstances, I should have my head examined."

"It was the champagne," she managed, wanting to explain her own unreasoning abandon, as well as his.

"Do you think so?"

"Yes."

Shifting his hands, he gripped her shoulders with tentative possession. "I've got some business at the downtown store in the morning. I won't be able to get back here until ten-thirty or eleven. Tell Miriam that, won't you?"

"Tomorrow?"

"If these papers don't happen to be the ones I need, she suggested driving to Belton. Remember?" He picked up the manila envelope.

"I remember," she whispered, sensing that things weren't over between them yet.

He smiled down at her, a high-voltage smile that zigzagged to her toes. "As long as we can blame it on the champagne..." Taking her trembling lips gently with his, he tasted them first, with the tip of his tongue, before kissing them tenderly. "Good night, Addie."

After he'd gone, she stood with her back against the door, listening to his footsteps recede. Then she walked slowly upstairs, stopping at Miriam's room to return the necklace. Miriam accepted it, smiling dreamily; she didn't seem inclined to talk, which suited Addie, who'd feared a barrage of questions about her feelings for Thorne.

The spell he'd cast lingered through her bath, feeding fantasies that rose above her like the steam from her perfumed tub. As she slipped into her nightgown with its dainty touches of ribbon and lace, her imagination played fully on the delicious possibilities of Thorne's reaction to seeing her in such a state of undress.

She gave her hair its nightly brushing, then paused, fluffing it, tousling it, and finally smoothing it to one side, wondering how she should wear it when she saw him again.

Not until she was cleaning her teeth did the truth strike her.

"I shouldn't have done that," Thorne had said. "I should have my head examined."

Why had he anguished over their kiss, unless he still believed that Addie was in Boston to get everything she could from her softhearted well-heeled relative?

Certainly Thorne's desire for her was real. No one could be that good an actor. But desire was all it was. Perhaps he'd even enjoyed their evening together. Perhaps he would enjoy their drive tomorrow. But his enjoyment was only part of it. He was prepared to go to any lengths to keep her busy. To give her as little opportunity as possible to work herself into Miriam's affections.

How could she have forgotten, even momentarily, the true reason behind his insistence on showing her the sights of Boston?

The schedule he'd set up left so little time for visiting that it rivaled the most rigorous schedules set by tour operators promising to show their customers fourteen cities in fourteen days.

Tomorrow? There could be no tomorrow for them, at least not the kind of tomorrow she'd temporarily allowed herself to visualize. What had happened between them tonight must not happen again.

CHAPTER FIVE

THEIR DESTINATION proved to be a Victorian-style farmhouse that must have been well over a hundred years old. Sand-colored, with orange doors and shutters, it sat in a large rectangular yard, hidden from the road by a tangle of wild roses and blueberry bushes.

The place had been a wedding gift from her father, Miriam explained. She and George had lived in it for the first ten years of their marriage. "Though I'll admit living in the city is more convenient, and I certainly enjoyed the place in Cape Cod, this has always been home to me. There are so many memories."

She showed Thorne the boxes she'd told him about, then sat down with Addie to go through old photographs.

"Oh, look. There's one of Thorne and George together," she cried, turning a page. "It was taken on the day Thorne graduated from law school. See how young he looks, and how proud? Talking about proud, look at George. Don't you think they resemble each other strongly? They truly could be father and son."

Addie nodded, not thinking so at all. Although George had dark hair, his features were far more pronounced and his build much heavier. Clearly Miriam wanted to see a resemblance, just as she wanted to believe she and Addie looked alike. Somehow, through the two of them, the old woman felt she might be able to relive her girlhood and the love she and her husband had known.

"And see this one." Miriam giggled. "It was taken at my christening. That's my mother in the huge beribboned hat. My father's in back, looking as if he's trying to hide. How he detested all the fuss!"

They were wonderful pictures, going back several generations, and Addie was so excited about them that she'd used three rolls of film before Thorne came in with the announcement that all was well. He'd found the documents he needed.

"Ready to start back?" He turned his wrist to look at his watch.

"Dear me, no!" Miriam cried. "I've had a lovely time. But I'm desperately in need of a nap. Do take Adeline and show her all our historical places and the poets' houses. When you're finished, you can come back for me."

"But wouldn't you rather I stayed and . . ." Addie began, panic rising inside her, as she wondered why she hadn't foreseen this.

"Good idea. Let's go, Addie." Before she knew what was happening, Thorne was holding her coat for her. She had little choice but to put it on.

Though she bristled as he ushered her out, she had a change of heart by the time they were on the road. It was right that Miriam should be allowed some time alone with her memories. Addie couldn't expect to hide behind the woman's skirts the whole time she was here.

Besides, she thought, maybe Thorne had already flexed his muscles and said what he had to say. For Miriam's sake, she'd allow him one more chance.

The drive was an enjoyable one, even though Addie suspected he would rather have been leading her on a safari into cannibal country.

"Driving used to have more of a kick to it," he said when they'd traveled a few miles in silence.

"Before the freeways?"

"Yep. Passing through tiny hamlets. Stopping at a roadside stand for an apple. Pulling in somewhere for a cup of coffee and talking about the weather with somebody else who's just passing through. Having to honk your horn to move a sleeping dog out of the road."

She wouldn't have thought he'd care about that sort of thing. "Sounds like slow going."

"Slow, but better. Mind if I open the window a few inches?"

"No, I like fresh air, too."

"And you've windproofed your hair." He gave her an approving nod. "I like it that way. It takes an exceptionally pretty face to carry off such severity."

When she'd sleeked it back, the caprices of the wind had only partly entered into her thinking. She'd also wanted Thorne to know that she went to no trouble to be attractive for him.

She'd worn her rust-colored pants with their matching jacket, along with a cream-colored cotton shirt. No frills. No baubles. No bangles or beads. The picture was supposed to say, *What you think of my appearance means less than nothing to me, Mr. Cameron. I have no intention of turning your head.*

She wouldn't snarl or show her teeth unless provoked. But she wouldn't feel called on to entertain him with witty repartee. He was transportation, nothing more. Being aloof wasn't easy, however. He was in a cheerful mood and had a lot to say about the happenings of that morning, and about their destination.

He talked about his affection for Miriam, too, about her late husband, George, and about how perfect the two had been together. Maybe too perfect.

"How can a husband and wife be too perfect together?" she asked, curious about his meaning.

"She was devastated when he died. Though I've heard doctors say there isn't such a thing, she had what's commonly called a nervous breakdown. She wouldn't go out or see anyone, and she'd still be in her housecoat at six o'clock in the evening, with no makeup, and her hair uncombed."

"That doesn't sound like Miriam."

"It wasn't Miriam. It was as if she'd died along with George. She'd been little more than a child when he married her, and he always saw her as a little doll to be pampered and protected from the cruel world. When he discovered that he had only months to live, he didn't give a damn about himself. His only concern was for Miriam. Who would look out for her when he was gone?"

And from what Addie could figure, Thorne had either been selected or had volunteered to watch over her. "He must have been a very special man."

"Yes. Very special." He gripped the steering wheel harder and stared at the road ahead with new intensity. "I feel honored to have known him."

There were other questions Addie would have liked to ask. How had Thorne come to know the Mandevilles? Why did he have such respect for George? How had their friendship come about? But the drive to Lexington, which Miriam had insisted they see, was a short one. The road signs had already announced their arrival.

"I'm sure you've read up on your history," he said as he angled the car precisely between the slanting white lines of a parking space. "There's no need to stop at the visitor's information center."

"Oh, but I want to." Her disappointment must have been evident, because he laughed a gentle unself-conscious laugh that caught her up and made her laugh, too.

"With all the snapshots you're taking of every stone and blade of grass, I wouldn't think you'd need any more souvenirs."

"True." She grimaced. "I've used so many rolls of film already, I'll have to mortgage the old homestead to pay for the developing."

Ouch. Cringing, she allowed him to help her out of the car. It was an innocent remark, but with his suspicious nature, he'd probably filed it away as Exhibit A, proving her guilty of hinting for a handout to help pay for the film processing.

Armed with literature and a map of the town, they began a self-guided tour. Except for its colorful past, Lexington might have been any other pretty little New England town, with its neat little shops, quaint clapboard houses and tree-lined streets.

"Ready to push off?" he asked, when they'd done everything on Addie's prepared list and stood on the Battle Green, looking up at the statue of the Minuteman.

"Can we stay a little longer and absorb the moment?"

"Absorb all you like. There's plenty of time."

"I wish Barney could have come along."

"Why didn't he?"

"He has arthritis, which keeps him from doing much walking, along with high blood pressure they haven't been able to stabilize yet. And there's the store to run. But he began a collection of miniature revolutionary-war soldiers when he was a boy."

Thorne gestured at the statue. "And you'd like to take this overgrown one back to him?"

She giggled. "Maybe."

The sunlight was strong on his face, showing the faint lines around his eyes and at the corners of his mouth. The glaring brightness gave his skin a rich glow, though it was too early in the year for a full-fledged tan. He had a wonderful face, full of character and pride. How easy it would be to get used to it. How easy to fall in love with the man behind it.

She hardly realized she was staring, until it struck her that he was staring back. It wasn't fair of him to wear blue. The pale hue of his shirt did something to his eyes, making it difficult for her to look away.

"I know I've made things unpleasant for you here, Addie," he said with a new gentleness, "and I suppose you despise me for it."

"You *have* made things difficult," she admitted, starting to walk again. "But despise is too strong a word."

He fell into step beside her. "I would guess that you feel things very strongly."

"I do. And I'll admit you haven't been my favorite person." She paused for a moment, then went on, deciding that since Thorne had opened the door for her questions, she might as well ask them. "I can't understand why you feel so protective toward Miriam. She's a strong woman. If she was a recluse for a time, as you say, well, she's recovered."

"That's true. But it wasn't only her withdrawal from the world that worried me. Later, when she began to see people again, it was partly because she'd found false hope in books on the occult. Inspired by them, she visited every so-called seer and fortune-teller in the city. She even attended séances, trying to receive messages from George. When I offered no encouragement and finally refused to go to any more of the sessions with her, she stopped speaking to me. During that time, she handed over a small fortune to one charlatan after the other."

"She didn't mention any of this in her letters."

"Fortunately she managed to find herself again. Appearances to the contrary, however, her emotional health is still fragile. I don't want anything to happen that might jeopardize it."

"You seriously believe I might hurt her?"

"I don't know what to think. But on the plus side, I do know that discovering you—the niece she didn't know she had—has helped to bring her back to herself better than any medicine could have done."

"Why should that be? She had Kevin."

"Yes, and she's fond of him. But he's a Mandeville, not a Rutherford. Her blood doesn't flow in his veins."

"That makes such a difference?"

"Yes, along with the fact that Kevin's been a disappointment to her. He doesn't give a damn about the company, and he seldom comes to see her. To his way of thinking, he has better things to do with his time than visit an old woman."

"He doesn't seem to be the neglectful sort."

"Would you say you've known him long enough to be a judge of that?"

"I suppose not." Who was Thorne, the master of snap judgments, to be asking such a question?

"Anyway, Miriam was amused and charmed by your letters. She even read some of them to me."

Addie's face warmed as she remembered the silly everyday things she'd written to fill up the pages. Miriam had remarked that she enjoyed long newsy letters, and so she'd tried to oblige. "They weren't meant for your eyes."

He shrugged. "There was nothing incriminating in them, was there?"

Incriminating? "Hardly. I write the way I feel."

"You write well. The stage was completely set for your arrival and you were perfect. Exactly what she would have wanted a niece to be. Young, vibrant, beautiful."

"You make it sound devious. They were only letters."

"But the timing was perfect. Whatever your motives for being here, you've helped her. I'm grateful for that."

Whatever her motives... Whatever her motives? That did it! She stopped walking and whirled around to face him squarely. "You aren't a stupid man, Thorne."

"Are you sure you can afford such an extravagant compliment?"

"You couldn't have made it through law school if you weren't above average in intelligence. I have a brother-in-law who did it, and while his personality leaves a lot to be desired, I have to admit he has a good brain."

"Is that right? Well..." Letting the word hang in the air, he glanced over his shoulder as if he thought the car might drive away without them.

"I also know words are part of your trade. Not just the words themselves, but the different meanings ordinary words take on according to the way they're said. According to the way pauses might be distributed. Invisible commas. Quotation marks."

"And?"

"And when you insult me, I know it isn't because you don't know any better. It's an insult by intent."

"Insult in the first degree." A smile twitched the corner of his mouth, belying his scowl. "I see."

"Good. Because I won't take it anymore. Another ugly insinuation, another slur, and I leave, even if I have to walk."

"And Miriam?"

"I'll make her understand somehow that neither of us is to blame. Our personalities clash and that's all there is to it."

"A failure to communicate?" From his blank expression it was impossible to tell his reaction to her ultimatum. He was studying her as if he thought he might learn something more just by looking deeply into her eyes.

"It's up to you. If you want to be friends, fine. If you're determined to be something else, you can darned well have that, too. Starting now. This minute."

She'd been prepared for a begrudging nod. Or maybe an angry tirade. But she hadn't expected him to laugh. Her words weren't selected to tweak his sense of the ridiculous, but apparently they did. In an effort to control his mirth, he turned away from her and shook his head.

"I'm glad you think it's funny." A tightening of her scalp signaled the rise of her blackest outrage.

"You've been here before, Adeline Rutherford," he said.

"No. I've never been to Massachusetts." Where was this new accusation headed? she wondered.

"You've been *here*. In this exact spot."

"What are you talking about?"

Confronting her again, he laid a hand on her shoulder and pointed to the stone marker almost at their feet. "Inscribed there are the words spoken by Captain John

Parker to the minutemen, moments before the battle. Read them."

"Why should I?"

He pointed again. "Humor me. Read it aloud."

"'Stand your ground,'" she read, with impatience at first, then more slowly. "'Do not fire unless fired upon. But if they mean to have war, let it begin here.'"

"'If they mean to have war, let it begin here,'" he repeated. "In essence, you chose the same spot to say the same thing."

Offering a reluctant smile of her own at the coincidence, she tilted her chin for an added show of determination. "And I meant it as much as he did."

"I know you did."

"Well?" He wouldn't wriggle out of this so easily.

"You're asking me to keep my opinions to myself?"

"You know exactly what I'm asking you. Do you find common courtesy so difficult?"

Irritation flashed across his face and he jabbed a finger at her. "This courtesy you're talking about works both ways?"

"Naturally."

For at least the count of ten, his eyes burned into hers, preparing her for a fresh assault. But then they softened. He extended a hand. "Okay, truce. Now are you ready to move on?"

When they'd checked off everything they wanted to see in Lexington, they drove to Concord, where they stopped at an ice-cream parlor for double-dip cones, and then at a souvenir shop, where Addie bought a Minuteman key chain for Barney. Afterward, they went for a stroll.

"Look there." Thorne came to a jolting stop in front of an art gallery. One of the paintings in the window showed a little girl of about four playing with a kitten.

"She reminds me of you. The round eyes, full of wonder. The delicate lips, ready to smile, but just as ready to pout. A little girl whose father couldn't deny her anything."

"You didn't know my father," she protested. " 'No' was his favorite word."

"But you didn't take no for an answer, did you?"

"That's another story." She smiled crookedly.

There was an awakening in the contact of their eyes this time. The casual sharing of simple things that day had allowed each to glimpse more deeply the inner being of the other. Thorne's answering smile faded slowly, leaving him with a questioning troubled look.

He cleared his throat and turned to the window again. "What do you think of that one?" He nodded toward the painting of a woman. Her hair, her clothing and the furnishings of the room were intricately detailed. But she had no face. It was called *Ideal*.

Luxuriating in his nearness, Addie fought the impulse to snuggle closer. She could almost tell the time by his face. By about five o'clock, it began to shadow again, needing a fresh shave. Shaking off the giddiness of discovery, she concentrated on what was supposed to be the object of her attention. The painting of the woman.

"The ideal woman has no face?" she asked huskily.

"The artist is allowing each man to envision his own ideal."

"Hmm." Addie preferred peaceful landscapes, or chaotic seas battering rocks, or homey Norman Rockwell scenes. "He took the easy way out."

"Not at all. Every woman is the ideal of the man who cherishes her."

"I wouldn't think you'd believe in that kind of thing— for every man there's a woman..."

"Every man holds an ideal."

And what's your ideal, Thorne? she wanted to ask, and likely did with her eyes. His hand slid down her arm and shifted, finding the curve of her waist. They began to walk again, aimlessly.

"A woman can have classically perfect features, alabaster skin and the carriage of a queen, and still leave a man cold," he said. "On the other hand, she can have the freckled turned-up nose of a twelve-year old, an undisciplined temper to match, and still drive him wild with longing."

The last of his speech jarred into place and spoiled the whole thing. He surely knew she was sensitive about the scattering of freckles across the bridge of her nose. She'd mentioned it to him before; he'd pretended not to notice, but had filed the remark away for future use. As for the rest of it, her temper was completely disciplined. Her outbursts, if they could even be called that, were justified.

"That's true," she said. "And a man can be overbearing, suspicious and egotistical, and a woman will still—" She stopped. When she'd begun the sentence, she hadn't thought how she would end it.

"And a woman will still . . . ?" he prompted.

"Will still be able to tolerate him."

He laughed. "That isn't what you planned to say."

"I have a habit of talking before I think. Especially when I'm with someone who dissects each word, examines it under a microscope and decides how to use it against me."

"Uh-uh." He slid his other arm around her and drew her closer. "Don't you remember our truce?"

"Do *you?*"

"Maybe I should kiss you to seal our bargain." His mere utterance of the word "kiss" sent a delicious shiver through her.

"It isn't necessary."

"I think it is." His hold on her was gentle, and when he pulled her closer still, he did so gradually, allowing her the option of refusal. A simple twist, one way or the other, would have freed her.

Only her sense of where they were made her draw back. "We can't. Not here."

"People don't kiss in Concord?"

"Not in the public square."

"Where then?" He looked around, plunging his hands deep into the pockets of his windbreaker. "The movie theater. Back row. When the lights go out?"

"It doesn't open until six-thirty," she said, laughing at his nonsense.

"We could rent a canoe and paddle upriver."

"It's getting late. Miriam will wonder about us."

Touching an index finger to a place below her ear, he traced her jawline. Back to her ear and down again once more, the faintly rough fingertip moved and came to rest beneath her chin. She drew a shaky breath and her lips parted in tingling expectancy. Passersby who might serve as an audience no longer mattered.

"You're right," he said, matching her sigh with one of his own. "We'd better go. It's starting to rain."

"It is?" She opened her eyes, not realizing until then that she'd closed them.

"Just a sprinkle." He held up one flat palm. "But it'll get worse. Come on.

"Would you like some music?" he asked when they were in the car again. He touched the radio dial.

"I don't care."

"Neither do I."

As the miles flew by she learned he shared her love of old movies. Tear-jerker dramas, Laurel and Hardy comedies, and cavalry-to-the-rescue westerns. He liked ice-skating, too, although he hadn't had skates on since he was nineteen. His favorite dessert was fudge cake and his favorite color was blue.

When the car came to a stop, she was taken by surprise. It didn't seem possible that they could have come so far so quickly. Not until they were walking hand in hand down the long curving driveway to the farmhouse did she begin to wonder why they hadn't parked closer. Then she didn't have to wonder.

With his fingers still twined tightly with hers, he led her off the path to a sheltered spot where a gnarled beech tree leaned at a perfect angle to support her as the length of his body pressed against hers. With a forearm resting on the trunk above her head, he brought his mouth a hair's breadth from hers.

"You knew this tree was here," she accused, feeling as if she were suspended above the Grand Canyon by a frayed thread.

"I always study the lay of the land." His lower lip jutted tentatively.

"It . . . it's stopped raining."

"So it has." Ducking his head, he murmured the words against the curve of her neck, nuzzling there to inhale the sweetness of her. "Tomorrow will be fair and warm."

"Thorne," she whispered, though she hadn't the strength to say anything more, or the clearheadedness to remember the comment she'd had in mind.

"Yes?" He outlined the rim of her ear with the tip of his tongue, which volleyed a thousand numbing joys through her limbs.

"Thorne!" she said again, louder this time, placing her hands on his chest as her strength waned.

"I'm right here, Addie. I'm not going anywhere." His voice was thick and strange. Shifting his weight, he took her face between his hands.

"You don't know how long I've waited for this. You bewitched me the moment you stepped off that plane and turned those golden eyes on me. I was all prepared to…"

"To hate me?" she managed.

"No, not to hate. To…I don't know. I can't think back that far."

"Neither can I."

"So if you have any objections to being kissed, speak now or—"

Unable to finish, he emitted a low moan, pulled her into his arms and opened his mouth over hers. His lips were soft, yet demanding. They were gentle, yet offered no mercy. His tongue was coaxing, yet relentless. It wasn't a long lingering kiss. It was many ever-deepening ones, which took complete possession. The impact was so intense, they might have been ill-fated lovers in another lifetime, separated by the ages and fearing something might now come between them.

When it was over, his hands slid beneath her jacket to burn her skin through the thin cotton of her shirt. Her fingers worked at his neck, delighting in the dark curling hair, the muscles and tendons beneath her fingers.

At last, set into motion by a new fall of gentle rain, they started toward the house. Neither spoke as they prepared themselves to talk about their day with Miriam.

When they reached the porch, Thorne squeezed her hand, and she squeezed back, smiling up at him. Yet inside her, a secret fear was building.

Thorough as his kisses had been, they hadn't been nearly enough. They had been only small tastes of what was probably to be a passionate insatiable hunger. Would that hunger ever be satisfied?

Yes, they'd made their truce. They'd touched on the problems between them. Yet nothing had been settled. No matter how hard she tried to convince herself otherwise, she knew a devastating clash was inevitable.

CHAPTER SIX

ADDIE HAD ALREADY SETTLED at the breakfast table with tomato juice and toast when Miriam swept in, looking perturbed.

"I'm afraid you'll be stuck with me today, darling. Thorne had to fly to Albany to tie up some business Kevin left untied. He won't be back for a few days."

"Stuck with you?" Addie unfolded her napkin carefully and placed it on her lap, using the action to hide her true feelings. "You're the reason I'm here, remember?"

She'd awakened that morning brimming with happy anticipation. On the drive back from Belton, Thorne had suggested taking a boat tour of the harbor, and it looked as if they had a glorious day for it.

"It could have waited," Kevin growled, following Miriam into the room. "Cameron never misses a chance to appear indispensable."

"It wasn't like that," Miriam assured him. "He simply thought—"

"I *know* what he thought."

Addie's disappointment at not seeing Thorne was so bitter, it gave her pause. How could she possibly feel so close to a man she'd known for such a short time? Why should it mean so much to her to be with him?

Maybe it was good that this had happened. She needed time away from him in order to stand back and take a look at their relationship, if it could even be called that at this early stage. Would Thorne—wherever he was—be thinking the same thing? Their hours together in Lexington and Concord had allowed her to see a highly appealing and extremely likable side of him. Had he, too, revised his opinion of her?

The trick would be to keep busy, and so she did. Comparing family notes, making corrections in the genealogical charts, and just chatting with Miriam filled up the first day.

The following morning she called Barney again to bolster his spirits after another strikeout in his quest for a loan. Then, gaining permission to borrow Miriam's car, she armed herself with pencils and notebook, and set off for Harvard.

"I'll be fine," she assured her aunt as she left. "We Rutherfords are born explorers. I'll be back by four."

"Promise to call if you have the slightest difficulty," Miriam said, probably torn between concern for Addie's safety and the desire to get her out of the house for the day.

Though Addie had pretended not to hear the whisperings, she was aware that the caterer in charge of Friday night's dinner party would arrive soon. Miriam, with typical childlike enthusiasm, wanted the details to be a surprise.

"I promise."

Though the worst of the morning rush was over, there was still enough traffic to keep her mind on the business of driving, as she took the bridge across the Charles River into Cambridge.

The Harvard library had a genealogy section that was everything it was purported to be. She found several tidbits about Isaiah, as well as references to two other Rutherfords she'd never heard of before—Nate and Jeremiah. As an unexpected bonus, while searching the medical archives, she found a copy of a thesis written in 1865 by a later Jeremiah for his doctorate in medicine.

That night, to celebrate her discoveries, Kevin escorted her and Miriam to an elegant French restaurant. From there, they attended a showing one of his friends was having in the artists' quarter. Afterward, there was a cocktail party at another gallery. It took time to pry Kevin away from the bar, and when Miriam finally managed it, a lengthy argument ensued over his ability to drive. Addie eventually took the wheel, but it was quite late by the time they returned home.

When she came down to breakfast on the third morning of Thorne's absence—she'd caught herself counting the days that way—she found only Kevin, who was staring glumly into his coffee cup, evidently suffering from the effects of last night's celebrating. Miriam, wearied from their long evening, was sleeping in.

"Ready for Auntie's big bash?" he asked, valiantly brightening for her sake. "From what I've heard it's going to be the dinner party of the decade."

She grimaced. "As ready as I'll ever be."

"The two of you are going shopping this afternoon, I hear. Why not take her somewhere special for lunch while you're about it?"

"Good idea." She poured a glass of orange juice and sat beside him. "Is there a restaurant you could recommend—one she especially likes?"

He frowned in concentration. "I don't know. I lean toward Thai food. Auntie detests it." He took a sip of coffee. "Wait. She keeps a notebook in the side table. It has jottings about her favorite things. Department stores, beauty salons. Look at the last page. I believe she's listed a few of her favorite restaurants. You could choose one and surprise her.''

''Wonderful. That sounds exactly right.''

''The one with the blue cover,'' he said, as she got up to search through the drawer he'd indicated. ''Pick a nice tearoom downtown—she adores those places.''

Addie ran a finger down the list. ''She's marked one with two stars. Madame Cassandra's Tearoom, on Arlington.''

He frowned. ''Ah, yes. I know the place. Good choice.''

''Do you know how to get there?''

''No problem. Here.'' He drew a ballpoint pen and a matchbook out of his pocket and sketched a map on the cover. ''You know the Public Gardens?'' When Addie nodded, he traced a path with his pen. ''Make a right here, a quick left, and there you are. Madame Cassandra's is in the middle of the block.''

''Is the food good?''

''Miriam loves it.''

''Then it's decided.''

THE COPLEY PLACE MALL was a city in itself. Beautifully designed to reflect the character of the historical surroundings, it extended for blocks, with an enormous waterfall, pink marble floors and more elegant stores than it would have been possible to explore in a dozen visits.

Miriam led the way from one shop to another, seeming to sense at a glance if a place contained anything to her liking. When at last she chose a dress, she asked Addie to model it, so she could see how it ''moved.'' Then she might decide to buy it to wear at the upcoming dinner party.

If Addie hadn't been worried about Barney, wanting to call him again to see how things were going, yet knowing he might see the constant checking on him as a lack of confidence—or if she hadn't been distracted by thoughts of Thorne, resenting his attitude toward her and at the same time missing his company—she might have realized at once what was happening. It wasn't until Miriam coaxed her to model a stunning sea-blue evening dress that the the truth struck home.

"You and I aren't the same size or coloring," she protested. "And you said you hate yourself in blue."

Miriam tittered behind her hand. "Very well. I'll confess. It's for you."

"Oh, no!" Addie was adamant about not accepting the dress, but Miriam was just as immovable. Why should she be comfortable financially if she wasn't allowed to use her money to buy things that brought her pleasure? Thorne guarded her investments like a fire-breathing dragon, and she wasn't supposed to sell stick or stone of what she had, or make any major purchases, without consulting him. Now everyone else, including her beloved newfound niece, was trying to prevent her from making small insignificant ones.

"Insignificant? A handkerchief in this shop would cost more than I'm used to spending on an entire outfit."

"Piffle! It's important to me that you look radiant for our guests on Friday night. Everything you have is so…"

"Drab?" Addie finished for her.

"Not drab exactly. Yes. Drab. Please humor me this one time. Do you imagine my buying that teeny little dress will send me into bankruptcy?"

In the end, faced with the prospect of tears she knew Miriam could summon at will, Addie relented. One dress. If it ended there. What harm could it do? Besides, she had to admit her refusal had been partially based on Thorne's reaction to an expensive gift. Why should she allow that to influence her? If he wanted to go on thinking the worst of her, he had no place in her life now or ever.

Pleased at getting her way, Miriam didn't ask where they were going, as Addie followed the map she'd memorized to the tearoom.

"Oh, darling. Madame Cassandra's," the woman cried, as they pulled into the parking lot. "It's been ages and ages since I came here. How did you know about it?"

"I looked through your address book," Addie admitted. "I hope you don't mind."

"Mind? How could I? Oh, my. This makes my day."

If there were anything special about the restaurant, it was that there *was* nothing special. Its ordinary exterior was topped only by its ordinary interior. An unpleasant pungent odor tickled Addie's nostrils. If that was what was cooking, she was sure she wouldn't be able to eat it.

Her first thought was that the stars in Miriam's book had meant thumbs-down, and that the older woman was only pretending to be pleased. Should Addie take the lead and suggest they leave before they were shown to one of the plain wooden tables in the dismal-looking dining room?

It was too late.

"Mrs. Mandeville, how good to see you." The man who greeted them wore golden earrings and a bright red shirt with wide sleeves. "We've missed you. Come. We'll seat you at your usual table."

Her *usual* table? Did that mean Miriam actually had come here more than once?

"You won't be disappointed," the older woman promised her, her eyes shining. "It will be an experience you'll remember."

Addie didn't doubt that. No menus made an appearance, but after a few minutes, a boy brought them steaming cups of tea and backed away again, without looking at them. Not fond of tea, Addie always took it with sugar. There was none on the table.

"Drink," Miriam coaxed, sipping her own. "You must."

Must? The brew was bitter, and so strong it brought tears to her eyes. If the scene had been in a movie, she thought, this was the point where the comedian would distract his companion by pointing at something across the room, while he poured his drink into a potted plant.

As she inhaled, strengthening herself for a long drink, a veiled woman dressed in black swept over to their table and sat down without a word. Taken by surprise, Addie set her cup back in its saucer. The outfit was nothing if not overkill.

"Madame Cassandra," Miriam whispered.

"You wish a 'life reading' for this girl."

"Yes. Yes, I do."

"I knew you would come," the woman said. "I have been waiting." Carefully she unwrapped something that looked like a flat round cracker and held it out for Miriam to take a bite. Then she held it out to Addie, who followed suit. That done, she crumbled the rest into bits, and scattered them on the table. With her eyes closed, she began to chant.

"She has been close to you for a very long time, this girl," the woman said at last. "A very long time."

Strike one, Addie thought, tempted to explain that she and her aunt had just met. She was stopped by the enthralled expression on Miriam's face.

"I see you together, laughing, sharing many joys. Many sadnesses. Woven together in the threads of other lifetimes."

"Yes," Miriam whispered.

"There was a break—here. One that came too soon. Much too soon. How is not clear. Much has gone between. The intervention of death, perhaps. Then, by chance, your lives crossed again—here. Do you see?"

Miriam inhaled sharply. "Yes."

When she was in high school, Addie had gone to a fortune-teller with her friends. She'd guessed easily how it worked then, and what this woman was doing now was just as clear, as the supposed reading progressed. She was using what she'd already learned about Miriam during other visits as a base. Now she was reaching out for something new, something that would include Addie, testing for reaction, backing off if she was wrong and elaborating when she'd accidentally struck the truth.

"Love is still a powerful force in your life. Time has not changed this. The man—the older man who was your husband—is still beside you. When last we met, his image appeared to be fading. Now it is strong again. Very strong."

"Yes, yes."

"He is pleased that you have picked up the silver threads of your destiny again. That you have someone by your side now, to help weave the new with the old. Do not fight it. Allow yourself to flow with your feelings."

Addie wanted to laugh. The seer's words sounded like the lyrics of a popular song. But when she looked at Miriam again, she no longer felt amused.

Her aunt was pale. Her hands, clasped on the table, were trembling. Her breathing was shallow. On and on the seer droned, passing on supposed messages from George Mandeville, suggesting that he was with them now and approved of this attempt to "look beyond the many veils of this world."

"We'd better go," Addie said suddenly, worried.

Miriam didn't reply. It was as if she were hypnotized.

"She is thinking of things that were. Things that will be," the seer said. "That is all."

"It *isn't* all. Miriam, can you give me your doctor's phone number?" It might be wise to make arrangements for him to be waiting when they got home, Addie thought.

"Let Madame Cassandra finish." Miriam's voice was a childlike whine.

"She *is* finished. Excuse us, Madame Cassandra." With some difficulty, Addie managed to get Miriam to her feet and slip her coat on.

"You should not leave now. I see other things. Many other things." The seer's pale eyes hardened.

"Then how is it you can't see that Mrs. Mandeville isn't well?" Addie snapped, leading Miriam to the door. "I'm sure she'll see that you get your fee later."

CHAPTER SEVEN

"WANT SOME COMPANY?" Kevin asked, coming up behind her as Addie put on her coat.

"Frankly, no," she said, stiffening.

Though Miriam was fine, according to the doctor, and he'd prescribed only a mild sedative, she still felt responsible for what had happened. After what Thorne had said about the woman's consuming interest in the occult, she should have insisted on leaving as soon as she discovered that Madame Cassandra was a fortune-teller.

Now she only wanted to get out of the house for a time. To the library? No. She wasn't in the mood for research. To the park? Yes. She'd sit and watch the joggers. Maybe she'd buy a bag of peanuts and feed the squirrels.

"I'm sorry about what happened," Kevin said.

"Are you?" She looked at him squarely.

"I had no idea what kind of joint that tearoom was. I only knew Auntie used to go there quite a lot. Don't you believe me?"

"Does it matter?"

"Yes, it does."

He looked so genuinely unhappy that she decided not to make an issue of the trouble his advice had caused. There was always a possibility that he was telling the truth.

"Very well. I believe you." What point would there be in holding a grudge?

"Prove it. Let me take you wherever you're going."

"I don't think so."

"You haven't seen Boston until you've taken a turn on Beacon Hill. No seamy side lanes. No sordid tales. I promise."

"I'm rather tired. The shopping. The scene at the tea-room..."

She'd definitely lost her knack for saying no and meaning it, she thought later, as she and Kevin were zig-zagging up one steep street, and down another. Or maybe it was just curiosity that made her decide to spend some time with him.

Was he really as friendly as he pretended to be, or did he resent her as much as Thorne did? Did he have an-other cruel prank in mind? In any case, she'd be on the alert, and as an added attraction, she'd see Beacon Hill.

Or maybe she should say that she'd "experienced" it. The rich redbrick houses, with their gleaming brass knockers, the cobblestones and shimmering gaslights made her feel she'd turned a corner from the present to the past.

She also learned something more about Miriam as they strolled together at a much more leisurely pace than she and Thorne would have taken. Something that helped her understand why the woman had been so thrilled to un-cover a new branch of the family tree.

Illness, misfortune and even war had taken their toll on the Boston Rutherfords over the years. Miriam's only brother had been killed on Iwo Jima in World War II, and his son had died in a helicopter crash in Vietnam. He'd had no children.

"Finding out about you gave her life new meaning," Kevin went on. "I'm only surprised Cameron has been so attentive. His nose is likely out of joint."

"Why do you say that?"

"He's the son Miriam and George never had. While he was never officially adopted—his own parents are still alive—he might as well have been, for the way they took him into their house, and more than that, into their hearts. With his lack of background, could he have slid into any other company as big and prestigious? Would any other firm have allowed him such complete control? Hell, no. It was George's affection for him that did it. I imagine your sudden appearance put a definite crimp in his plans."

"What plans are those?"

"Oh, to get his hands on the Mandeville fortune for one thing. To impress his ex-wife enough that she might come running back. You knew he'd been married, I suppose."

Married? Thorne? She stopped walking. "No, I didn't."

Why was she so surprised to hear of it? At thirty-six, it would have been natural that he'd found someone. But why did the news bother her so much? Maybe it was because during those hours they'd spent sight-seeing, they'd told each other so many things that she'd begun to believe she knew him completely. How could he have left out something as important as an ex-wife?

"The marriage didn't work out, and it's a sensitive subject for him," Kevin went on, not noticing her reaction to the bomb he'd dropped. "She's a mile above him on the social scale, and as ambitious as she is beautiful. My understanding is she married Cameron, expecting him to go far. It rankled her that he attached himself to the Mandevilles and wouldn't go through any of the doors her father opened for him. She didn't have the patience to wait until George and Miriam died to start living the way she'd always lived."

How calculating it sounded, put that way. Was it true that Thorne's affection for Miriam was all show? "I still don't see why he should resent me."

"Maybe he doesn't resent you personally. Just the bite he's afraid you'll take out of the Mandeville holdings."

"I don't want anything from Miriam," she said with uncharacteristic sharpness, because she felt accused once again.

"Can Cameron be sure of that? The Rutherford blood runs in your veins, not his, George and Miriam's affection for him notwithstanding. And more than that, will your wishes keep Miriam from including you in her new will?"

"Wills, inheritances." She almost wished the older woman had truly been the shopkeeper's widow she'd expected to find when she'd arrived in Boston. "What about people, feelings, love? Doesn't any of that count?"

"Maybe I shouldn't have told you."

"I'm glad you did. It explains a few things." Thorne's protectiveness toward Miriam's fortune, for instance. How dared he superimpose his greed on her!

"How good are you at throwing darts?" Kevin asked unexpectedly as the cab they'd taken home—at her insistence—pulled up to the curb. "You don't want to go in yet. Let me take you to a genuine Irish pub. A favorite spot of mine."

"Not this time, thanks. I want to make sure Miriam's all right." She paid the driver without comment, since Kevin didn't seem to be in any hurry to reach for his wallet.

"Not *this* time?" Kevin, who'd worn a bulky hand-knit sweater instead of a coat—trying to be a "hero," as

Barney would have put it—rubbed his arms briskly to warm them before opening the cab door for her. "Can I take that to mean we'll do this again?"

"If you like," she told him, the reality of their spending more time together seeming too vague and distant to worry about. The here and now, the fortunes of the moment, were too precarious.

On the other hand, maybe she should consider his offer to be her escort. If Miriam saw them together a few times, she might abandon the idea of pairing her up with Thorne.

They moved down the corridor to the music room, where the maid said Mrs. Mandeville might be found waiting for them before going in to dinner. As they approached, Addie heard voices. Suddenly she felt as if an icy hand had clapped her on the back of the neck.

Thorne had returned. Called back early because of the incident at the tearoom?

She didn't have to wonder if he'd heard about her latest sins. His devastating glare as she and Kevin walked in was all the assurance she needed.

Miriam, looking rather pale, was dressed in a soft shade of gray, with a rose chiffon scarf at her neck to add color. All through dinner, she chatted animatedly about Thorne's success in heading off a lawsuit at the Albany offices.

"You never cease to amaze me, darling." She rested a frail hand on his arm. "George couldn't have handled things better himself."

Another candy company had claimed that Mandeville's new ad campaign, already saturating the airwaves, had been stolen when an irate employee left them and joined the Mandeville team.

"I had everything well in hand," Kevin protested. "It was a matter of letting things cool."

"Cool? It was heating up to the point of explosion." Characteristically, Thorne's voice was more controlled when he was angry.

"I know these people," Kevin shot back. "I've dealt with them for years."

"Then why didn't you stay with it?"

"Maybe you'd like it if I stayed in Albany permanently."

"Hardly. I'd hate to see New York go down the tube."

"Enough business talk," Miriam broke in. "Why don't we go back to the music room and have our coffee there?" Winking at Addie, she took Thorne on one arm, Kevin on the other, and all but pulled the two men along.

Thorne, clearly, would have liked to escape, but felt called upon to humor her after her ordeal. Kevin, who took his glass of wine with him, probably went to defend himself, in case the other man said something derogatory.

"I've already received telephone confirmations for every one of my dinner invitations," Miriam announced brightly, when they were settled. She rested a possessive arm on Thorne's shoulder. "Everyone is dying to meet the new addition to the clan."

"Addie won't disappoint them. A very lovely addition she is." Kevin crossed to refill his glass. "You two must have bought out the stores today, setting her up with a new wardrobe. The floor-to-ceiling boxes got home before you did."

Oh, no, thought Addie. Miriam didn't. She wouldn't. She hadn't bought all those other outfits she'd had Addie model, had she? She'd promised she would buy only the one dress. Addie tried to catch the older woman's eye for reassurance, but Miriam seemed intent on signaling her nephew to hold his tongue.

"Poor Addie brought a suitcase full of clothes from California," he went on, his tongue loosened by the wine he'd downed. "But nothing suitable, I gather. It's the way people dress out there. Their idea of formal attire is a rhinestone patch on the seat of their skintight Levis."

"Kevin!" Miriam gasped.

He grinned. "I'll admit it sounds fetching, at that."

A bitter taste filled Addie's mouth. She felt as if her face were a mask, set in a blandness of expression she didn't feel. Since her arrival, she'd been insulted repeatedly by Thorne, and from the look of things, the worst was yet to come. She'd been led into a trap by Kevin. Now she'd been deceived by Miriam.

She imagined herself screaming and running from the room, throwing her things into a suitcase and catching a cab to the airport without any explanations. Her place was with Barney, anyway.

Instead, she kept quiet, withdrawing from the conversation entirely, listening to the cadence of the voices without hearing what was said. She concentrated on the unique furnishings of this, her favorite room in the house. Here was a Tiffany dragonfly lamp. There was a silk fan encased in glass, and next to it a tasseled parasol. In a special carved niche in the wall opposite her was a nearly life-size doll with staring glass eyes. On a shelf above it sat a pair of glass slippers, and a bit beyond, on the same wall, hung a floppy, wide-brimmed hat with a pink velvet ribbon. Had Miriam worn it as a girl? Had she carried the parasol, played with the doll?

Thorne's voice drew her attention. He had been summoned to the telephone. Miriam had brought out her leather case of old photographs and was showing them to a bored Kevin, who cared only that his glass was filled.

Seizing the moment, Addie mumbled something about the powder room and made her escape. Down the corridor she went, her steps soundless on the lush carpeting, as she sought the sanctuary of the side terrace.

After the warmth of the music room, the cool night air made her shiver. The radio had predicted rain. She doubted it. The sky was purple velvet, sprinkled with rhinestone stars—or rather, in the case of any stars that would dare to twinkle over the Mandeville house, diamond ones.

She stood at the railing, looking out at the beautifully landscaped yard, lit here and there with colored lights. Though the grounds were comparatively small, room had been found for a tiny gazebo, and off to one corner, an iron deer, which Addie had at first glance supposed was real.

Her hands gripped the icy metal as the door opened and a shadow fell across the floor tiles. Sensing it was Thorne before he spoke, she didn't look around.

"How did you find me?" she asked.

"You passed the door while I was on the phone. And in rather a hurry. I wanted to talk to you."

Her throat tightened. "About what happened today? Go ahead and say it."

"I will. What the hell were you trying to do? I warned you about Miriam's obsession with psychics."

"Would you recognize the truth if you heard it?"

"Are you capable of telling it?" He moved beside her. "I felt very close to you that day we spent together in Concord. I was warmed by the things you said and impressed by the person I began to believe you were. When I was in Albany, I had a devil of a time concentrating on business, because I was thinking about you. Remembering how you smiled. How good I felt when you were in my arms. Wanting to have you there again. Wondering if I'd misjudged you. Wondering how I could make it up to you."

She felt as if she were made of chalk. At any moment, she would crumble. If he'd begun to care, if he'd begun to sense the special magic between them, as she had, how could he thrust it away at the first sign of misunderstanding?

"And...and now?"

"Now I don't know what to think. No matter what I feel for you, dammit, I have an obligation to Miriam, and I don't intend to let you exploit her."

"Is that what I'm trying to do?"

"You made good use of my absence, didn't you?" His voice dropped an octave with his contempt. "This last trick was unconscionable. Didn't you consider the damage you could have done? And it was so unnecessary. You were already 'in' with her. She already sees herself in you."

Addie glared at him, grateful for the accusation that allowed her hurt to give way to outrage. "That's what you think today was about? My trying to be 'in' with her?"

"What else? Since I arrived this evening, she hasn't been able to stop telling me what this soothsayer told her about your life being linked with hers. About George watching over both of you, comforted that you've come into her life."

"Am I responsible for what the woman said?"

"I wonder. I've been told that a phone call in advance to set things up, accompanied by crossing the palm with silver, can map out a touching scenario."

If he believed she was capable of such treachery, there was no hope at all that they could smooth out their differences. "I won't bother trying to explain. It isn't important whether you belive me," she said simply.

"I suppose not." He gripped the rail and looked out at the garden, too. "As long as it's understood that if there are any further occurrences of what happened today, I won't be responsible for the consequences."

"Should I be frightened?" She interjected a melodramatic quiver into her voice.

"If I were your attorney, I'd strongly recommend it." He allowed a long silence to reinforce his meaning. "Now, while you're here, there's something else I want to discuss with you."

"I can't wait to hear what it is."

"I have business in Amesbury. Not pressing. But I thought if I did it, say on Monday, you could ride along. We'd stop at Salem and see the sights."

"*You* thought?"

He offered a disarming smile. "Okay. Miriam suggested I take you. But I think it's a good idea."

How incredibly masculine he was, and tempting. Even in the casual tan corduroy jacket he wore, likely dropping everything when he received the call from the doctor or one of the servants to hurry back and help smooth over the results of Addie's treachery.

"Don't change your plans on my account," she managed, looking away from him again.

"I think you'd find Salem interesting."

"I'd find it disturbing," she shot back. "I know exactly how those women must have felt back then, being falsely accused of witchcraft."

A scowl lurked behind his smile. "History has exaggerated the happenings in Salem."

"Tell that to the poor people who were tried and convicted."

"The trials were held only in a single year and those found guilty were hanged, not burned."

"Oh, that's all right then, isn't it?"

He held his hands up in a gesture of surrender. "I wasn't among the judges, Addie."

"Maybe not. But if you'd lived in Salem then, you probably would have carried the rope."

"Now who's making false accusations?"

A trickle of perspiration ran down between her breasts, despite the cold, as she remembered the warm wonderful pressure of his hungry mouth on hers. The trip to Salem with him would guarantee more such kisses, and oh, how she wanted them. He'd talked about how good he'd felt when she was in his arms. Didn't he know how good she'd felt being there? He'd admitted he was beginning to care for her. Riding those long miles together could well recapture that caring. But if it did, it would be against his better judgment, and she wasn't interested.

"I want to thank you for your offer," she said, before she could change her mind. "But I've made other plans."

"Other plans. I see." His fingers drummed against the rail. "I'd take care what I was doing before I started up with Roper. He isn't all he seems."

"None of us are."

"His own father's given up on him. When the old man retired and sold his end of the business to George, he stuck Kevin in as part of the package. He hoped George might be able to do something with him. Make him take as much interest in the company as he did in the bottle."

"From what I've seen of Kevin, he acts the way people expect him to act. Have you ever tried showing a bit of confidence in him?"

"How can you show confidence in someone who doesn't give a damn? Yes, he's intelligent. Yes, as you've no doubt discovered, he can be personable. He could be an asset to Mandeville if he put forth some effort. As it is, he can't be trusted. With him, it would be caviar today. Hamburgers tomorrow."

"I like hamburgers."

There was nothing more to be said between them. Surely he knew it. Why didn't he just leave?

"Where did the two of you go earlier?" His voice had an edge to it.

"We took a walk."

"A bloody long one."

Was he actually jealous? Not likely. It was only that Kevin wasn't his favorite person. Perhaps he felt Kevin was a threat to his position in Miriam's affections, too. That was why he leapt on every opportunity to belittle the other man.

"I had a good time," she said.

"I could tell that by the way you looked when you came in. Radiant, but breathless. Did you forget to wear lipstick, or did you leave it on him?"

She ignored the gibe and gestured with one hand, trying to find words that would sound enthusiastic. "I forget what he has planned for tomorrow. But it'll be somewhere interesting."

"I can imagine. I take it I'm fired as a tour guide, then."

"You needn't bother with me anymore, if that's what you mean."

He reached out to her, and she pulled back instinctively, fastening him with a glare.

"You've something caught in your hair," he explained, removing a bit of leaf from her hair. "You probably brushed against the potted tree as you came through the door."

Or else he was performing magic, plucking the leaf from a place it had never been, only as an excuse to touch her and watch her reaction.

"Thank you."

"All the time I was away, I kept thinking about how it would be when we were together again." He dropped the leaf into the shadow made by the rosebush below. "I missed you."

"I imagine it was difficult to find someone who would stand still for your insults."

"It hasn't all been bad, has it? When things are good between us, they're very good."

"And when they aren't?" Her laugh was brittle.

"I wasn't trying to be amusing."

"What you said just reminded me of something—my first Thanksgiving dinner after my folks left the country. I tried so hard, but everything was horrible. The turkey was overcooked. My yeast rolls didn't rise. A disaster. When I started to cry, wailing that even my mashed potatoes were a failure, Barney put his arms around me. 'Heck, honey,' he said. 'Those potatoes were downright delicious—between the lumps.'"

With a sigh, she moved away from the railing and Thorne, and gazed through the glass doors, readying herself to go back inside.

"That's what our relationship has been," she said in a voice that was little more than a whisper.

"Delicious between the lumps," he repeated in a monotone. "I see. Still, there's more to see in Boston."

"I'll see it."

"But not with me." When she didn't answer, he took a step toward her. "There's unfinished business between us, Addie. Something that has nothing to do with Miriam, or with your reasons for being here."

"And that is?"

"You know damned well what it is. I see it every time you look at me, trying to pretend you aren't. I can sense the fight you're having with yourself—just as I am. I can feel the blaze of your desire as keenly as I feel my own."

"You're suggesting we warm ourselves in that blaze as long as it lasts?"

"Your words, not mine."

"But your sentiments, counselor. I'm fine, it seems, when there's just the two of us, alone together in the dark. What happens when the sun comes out?"

"Dark or light. Sun or moon, I've seen that same invitation in your eyes. An invitation no man could ignore."

His eyes skimmed over her, lingering many long seconds. She felt herself melting. In another moment there'd be nothing left of her.

"You have a vivid imagination, and a gigantic ego. I'm going in now. It's getting cold."

"You know you don't want to do that."

His hand shot forward, but she was ready for it. She pulled back in time, emitting a small cry of triumph. His other hand tried to snake around her waist, but she managed to evade it, too, twisting to avoid the potted tree behind her.

Thorne moved at the same time, putting himself between her and the door, ending the match. She collided with him and they struggled—a soundless frantic struggle. His mouth began to bear down on hers and she felt as if her blood were smoking as it rushed through her veins.

"Why such a life-or-death protest?" he taunted, so harshly she could feel his breath against her lips. "If I kiss you, it won't be the first time."

"And it won't be the first time you've forced yourself on me, either."

His hold on her tightened, molding the yielding softness of her body with the hardness of his, inciting unbearable longing it was torture to restrain. "I can't remember having to use force."

"Then you have a convenient memory. I understand. Some men prefer taking a woman against her will. Go ahead. You're stronger than I am."

It was probably no more than a few seconds that he held her without saying anything, his face a mask of impotent fury, but it seemed longer. Addie didn't even realize he'd let her go, until his arms fell to his sides.

"I didn't think you were serious," he said. "I thought it was a game you were playing."

"You *would* think that."

He pressed the back of his hand to his mouth, his eyes fixed on Addie's fingers as they smoothed her disarranged blouse. "My God, you have me reduced to behaving like an adolescent boy who's just discovered girls."

"May I go in now?" Her lips burned from the kiss they had expected and hadn't received. The kiss they would never receive.

Thorne touched a finger to her shoulder and traced a line, almost regretfully, down her arm to her hand. "A final warning. Appearances are deceiving. Roper can be ruthless. If you think you've latched onto a winner in him, think again. He's here only because of Miriam's loyalty to family."

Her eyes widened meaningfully. "Just like me."

"Even that loyalty is wearing thin," he went on, ignoring her sarcasm. "When Miriam tires of it, he'll be out on his ear."

"Oh, shucks. You don't think I should start buying my trousseau then?"

A muscle twitched at his temple. "Judging by what I heard inside about your shopping trips while I was gone, you already have. And with Miriam's money."

She brushed back a strand of hair that had fallen over her eyes during their struggle. "I won't try to explain that, either."

"You're right." He strode past her to the door and opened it, without looking at her. "It *is* cold out here."

CHAPTER EIGHT

THE SWEEPING VIEW of Boston from high above should have been the exhilarating high point of Addie's sightseeing, but she could barely muster an enthusiastic thank-you for Kevin.

Afterward, she walked across the Common with him as she had done with Thorne, along the same streets and through the archway at Charles and Beacon. It wasn't the same.

The city seemed to have changed. At every turn buildings were going up or coming down. Workers were sandblasting walls or erecting wooden barricades prohibiting movement. True, the beautiful old churches still offered unique stained-glass windows as subjects for exciting snapshots, but she hadn't thought to bring her camera.

Maybe she'd left it home deliberately, subconsciously wanting no more reminders of what she'd found in Boston, then lost so easily.

Her feelings toward Kevin were mixed. While she was upset with him for his excessive drinking and insensitive remarks at dinner the night before, she felt sorry for him. It must have been difficult, knowing that he'd been merely tolerated by George Mandeville because he was part of a package deal, while Thorne—an outsider—had not only been welcomed into the company, but had been placed in the position of decision-maker.

It wasn't only sympathy for Kevin, though, that made her agree to spend the day with him. It was defiance of Thorne's warning, and the reaction she hoped to get from him when she announced her plans at breakfast.

It had worked. He'd glared at his plate, pretending he didn't hear their cheerful discussion. Not a stranger to that glare, however, Addie knew what was behind it. Though it would have been satisfying to believe that it was borne of jealousy, she knew better. Accustomed to telling everyone what to do and when to do it, he resented her not falling into line. Well, in the week that remained of her stay, he'd get used to it.

"Your days here are dwindling to a precious few," Kevin reminded her now, as they walked back to the car.

"So they are."

"Do I detect a note of regret?"

"Not really. I've had a good time, but my grandfather needs me."

"He's in poor health?"

"It isn't that. He's very active. In fact, he still runs the hardware store he ran when I was little. At least, for the moment."

"He's retiring?"

"Not voluntarily." She sighed. Retiring. Just the sound of the word and the thought of how it would sit with Barney sobered her.

"How's that?" Kevin persisted.

"His partner died unexpectedly." Briefly she told the tale of her grandfather's problems with the bank.

Kevin nodded. "It happens every day. People don't realize how important it is to get everything in black and white. If you expect to talk this brother-in-law of yours into signing for the old man's loan, I think you're being optimistic. Everybody looks out for number one these days."

It was odd hearing someone refer to her grandfather as an "old man." She'd never thought of him that way. "It won't be as difficult as convincing Barney to accept help in the first place. He wants to work things out for himself."

Kevin dug into his pocket for his car keys. "Are you sure Barney is the whole reason for your glum expression?"

She hadn't realized it showed. "What else?"

He squinted against the afternoon sun. "I thought you might be hurting over Cameron. You wouldn't be the first young innocent taken in by his courtroom manner."

"Hardly." She summoned a smile and hoped it would reach her eyes. "Isn't there something called vacation lag?"

"I think so. It comes over people when they've enjoyed about as much as they can stand."

"I guess I have it."

He snapped his fingers. "Then I have a cure. More of the same. What haven't you seen in Boston that when you get back to LA people will ask if you've seen, and you'll have to admit you haven't?" He ran all the words together, like a carnival barker.

She thought for a moment. There was nothing. If she never went sight-seeing again, it would be too soon.

"I've read there's an extraordinary aquarium here," she said hesitantly. It was early yet and she wasn't ready to go back and chance facing Thorne so soon. "It might be worth seeing."

"You've got it." He snapped his fingers again. "One aquarium coming up."

Just as she was beginning to relax and feel a camaraderie with him, he maneuvered the car into the underground garage of what was clearly an apartment building. Her feeling quickly evaporated.

This wasn't going to be a pass, was it? She hoped not. She wasn't up to it.

"What an unusual place to keep an aquarium," she said dryly.

"I rent an office here. It makes for more congenial entertaining than a cubicle in one of those black glass buildings. I thought you'd like to see it." He sounded offhand, making her wonder if she'd misjudged him. "You'll see your aquarium, I promise."

It wasn't an office, though she allowed that he might have conducted business of a sort there. The plush carpet was a screaming red. The walls were metallic paper. The paintings were jarring splotches of color, and a gigantic twisted iron sculpture acted as a divider between the living room and the area that held a desk and an oddly fashioned red object that might have been a telephone.

"This room suits you," she observed, tossing her coat on the couch.

"I'm not sure that's a compliment." He posed beside one of the paintings, whose subject was an open-mouthed green-and-blue man with bulging red eyes, and mugged.

She laughed. "I'm not sure it is, either."

"And there you have your aquarium." He gestured broadly toward a fish tank set into the inside wall. It was furnished with the usual ceramic bridges, mermaids and water plants. But there were no fish.

She wasn't alarmed. If she had him pegged correctly, a quick jab in the ego could squelch him if necessary.

She'd say she was hungry and suggest they go somewhere to eat. If he became difficult, she'd call a cab.

"Sit down and make yourself comfortable." The invitation, accompanied by an awkward embrace, caught her off guard and sent her toppling onto his lap on the couch. "Tell your troubles to Cousin Kevin."

"You aren't my cousin," she snapped, wrenching herself free.

"By marriage."

"Not even by marriage."

He yanked his tie off and tossed it onto the coffee table. "Okay, let's be honest with each other. Auntie is a pushover for family, and you're family. On the other hand, she's grown unaccountably attached to me. That puts us in opposition to each other."

She glared at him, the heat of indignation prickling her face. Could he possibly be saying what she thought he was saying? Was his doting affection for his aunt only a pose? If this was a sick joke, she would put him in his place. If he meant it, and his attentions toward Miriam were inspired by greed, she didn't even want to be in the same room with him. Not now. Not ever.

"If that's your idea of humor, it isn't funny."

"You're right. It isn't. Even with the money she's leaving to her favorite charities—the children's hospital, the homeless, stray animals—there's enough left over to stagger the imagination. Far be it for me to laugh at that. And have you stopped to think what an unbeatable team we'd be, you and I? The thought of our offspring, of the two bloodlines together in one package, would tickle Auntie silly." He shrugged out of his jacket and reached for her again.

Revolted, Addie peeled his hands away. "Don't touch me."

"What's this? You didn't act the part of prim Sunday-school teacher with Cameron, or he wouldn't have wasted so much time with you."

"That's none of your business!"

"No?" He opened a door built into the arm of the sofa and pulled out a bottle and two glasses. When she shook her head, he poured something amber into one glass and drained it. "What'd you do all those hours you spent together? Play gin rummy?"

She glanced at the phone. If he was going to start drinking this early in the afternoon, she had no intention of letting him drive her home. "Do you mind if I make a call?"

"Go right ahead."

In spite of his concurrence, before she'd made a move, he lunged. They pushed and pulled, twisted and tugged, and he ended up pinning her against the couch with his body. Even when his frustrated yank tore half the buttons off her blouse, he didn't stop.

"I keep a sewing kit in my top drawer," he muttered.

"I can see why," she snapped, her hands pushing futilely at his chest.

"That's cute." He brought his mouth down on hers so hard her lips were crushed painfully against her clenched teeth.

It was no use. Her unwillingness to cooperate only seemed to stimulate him. The smell of the liquor he'd downed, mixed with the too-sweet scent of his after-shave made her feel ill.

"Could we have some music?" she asked softly, forcing herself to relax in his arms.

As she'd hoped, he loosened his grip, imagining his devilish appeal had finally won her over. "Why not? Music soothes the savage beast."

"The savage *breast,*" she corrected. "However, in your case, maybe it *is* beast."

He laughed and pointed a finger at her. "What do you like? Highbrow stuff? Lowbrow? What's your pleasure?"

"You choose," she said demurely.

Smoothing his shirt in place, he lurched across the room to the stereo center, whistling "Lara's Theme."

During their struggle, her purse had fallen to the floor. Snatching it up, she inhaled deeply, pushed the coffee table at an angle with one foot to block her host's path and raced to the door, grabbing her coat on the way.

"Hey!" He dropped the tapes he'd been holding and started after her. Not noticing the repositioned table, he fell over it, and skidded into a rack of magazines, uttering a string of the blackest oaths she'd ever heard.

"Stupid bitch!" he shouted. "Don't think I'm going to chase you. You aren't worth it."

CHAPTER NINE

THE JOGGERS were out in force on the esplanade. There were a few older couples in spiffy matching outfits and men in tank tops with numbers on their chests. But most wore baggy sweat suits, as if running demanded looking as unattractive as possible.

The grass smelled sweet with spring. The river was a ribbon of gold satin. Fat pigeons who'd gathered at Addie's feet when she first sat on the bench, had strayed away, deciding she had nothing to offer. Now there was only a handful of little black-capped birds bathing in a dusty depression near her feet and chirping joyfully.

It was a busy time of the afternoon. Cars inched over the bridge and along Storrow Drive. People were anxious to get home after the day's work.

Addie had to get home, too. At least to the house that was home for the time she had left in Boston. But she hadn't figured out yet how she was going to manage that.

After fleeing from Kevin's apartment building, she'd tripped over a sprinkler and landed in a freshly dug flower bed. Her pants were muddy. The palms of her hands stung where they were skinned. She had only one button left on her blouse, and if it weren't for her coat, she'd be sitting there showing an expanse of lacy bra.

Her makeup pouch was missing. Undoubtedly it had fallen out when her purse had overturned on the floor. She'd have to buy a comb and some lipstick, then seek out a public rest room to make repairs before she faced Miriam.

Had she overreacted? Could she have reasoned with him and prevented things from getting so out of hand? No. His determination had been reinforced by greed.

At least, she should have refused to enter his apartment in the first place. Should have. Could have. Every decision she'd made lately had been wrong. Beginning with her decision to come to Boston.

"Addie?"

"Oh!" Her surprise at seeing Thorne made a squeak of the exclamation.

He must have followed her. People didn't run into each other in a city this size. And *if* he'd followed her, it was because he regretted what he'd said to her on the terrace the evening before. He realized that if there was a plot afoot to bilk Miriam out of her money, she had no part in it. She was so glad to see him she wanted to cry.

Pausing to allow her heart to slow its frantic beating, she brushed her gaze past him. There was a small boat, with two people in it, on the river. The man was rowing. The woman sat back, showing her mane of coppery hair to advantage.

"What happened to you?" Thorne growled.

"I . . ." She clutched the lapels of her coat and looked up at him. He was wearing a pale sweatshirt and Levis so faded they were almost white. He hadn't followed her. He jogged along the esplanade every evening when he had the chance, he'd told her.

Had her subconscious held that thought and brought her here, hoping for the best?

"Why do you ask?"

"Are you serious? Look at yourself."

She slapped at the air, trying for a gesture of nonchalance. "Don't stop jogging. Your heart rate'll slow."

"The devil with that." He sat beside her on the bench and stretched out his long legs.

Frank was a jogger, too. Doing four miles a day, rain or shine, was a ritual for him, and if forced to remain in one spot for a moment or two, he'd punch the air with his fists and run in place, afraid he'd lose the "aerobic benefits" of what he was doing.

Though Addie admired his determination, she'd never thought of him as sexy when he was puffing and drenched with perspiration. Why was it different with Thorne? With his hair moplike and flopping over his damp forehead, he was as desirable as ever.

The rowers were closer to the shore now. Though she still couldn't see their faces clearly, the unselfconscious way they behaved together, and the way they leaned forward now and then to touch, made her certain they were in love.

Thorne was watching them, too. For the same reason? No. He was awaiting an explanation where there was none.

"I was running," she told him. "And caught my shoe in one of those...those..."

He clamped his teeth together. "That bastard."

"Who?"

"You know damn well who. I saw you leave with Roper this morning. It doesn't take much brain power for me to figure out why you were running."

"What kind of birds are those?" she asked, wanting to change the subject, and at the same time somehow set things right.

"Chickadees."

"They're so brave. They hardly hop out of the way to let people pass."

He nodded. "They don't let the winter winds chase them south, either. Somehow they survive."

"I wish I had something to feed them." It wasn't working. This was the kind of desultory conversation two strangers might have while standing in line at the supermarket.

He must have felt the same way. He patted his forehead with the back of his hand. "I'd better get you home."

"How will I explain to Miriam why I'm with you instead of Kevin?"

"Still protecting him?"

"I'll be leaving next week." She almost added "for good," but it would have sounded too melodramatic. "Why should I leave behind bitterness in the family?"

"Are you sure that's the whole reason?" His hand moved toward her, making her flinch, but it was only to brush away some grass. "Come on. I'm taking you to dinner."

Her lips were parched and dry. "I'm not dressed for dining out and Miriam's expecting me."

"You're dressed fine for the place I have in mind. And I'll clear it with Miriam—without implicating Roper, if that's the way you want it."

She accepted his hand. "Where are we going? To one of those cafés with a flashing neon sign that says 'Eats'?"

"Close. I'm taking you to my apartment." He touched a finger to the tip of her nose. "Don't look so terrified. I'm a good cook."

If she'd looked terrified, it wasn't at the prospect of his cooking, and he knew it. It was at the thought of the two of them alone together in the same room. "What if Miriam looks out the window and sees us arrive?"

"I'll pull in the back way."

"Actually, I'm not very hungry."

"Liar." His eyes probed hers and held them. "We'll put our truce back in force."

"Some truce," she said under her breath, and he laughed.

The walls of his living room were white, which didn't quarrel with the hodgepodge of incidental color. Two of those walls were floor-to-ceiling books. The third had a slim racing bike hung on it, and along the fourth stood a music center, with a stereo and a staggering record collection. Above it was a Glen Miller poster and a crossed pair of dueling swords. The coffee table was a glass-topped boulder, and an antique sundial and a bottle with a sailing ship inside sat on a portable television.

"No, I didn't," he said, coming up behind her to take her coat and toss it onto the back of a chair.

"Didn't what?"

"Put the ship inside the bottle."

She smiled despite herself. "I didn't think you did. You don't have the patience."

He lifted the toffee-brown weight of hair at the back of her neck. "My patience might surprise you."

Suddenly he noticed the way she was clutching the front of her blouse. "Roper?" At her flush and embarrassed nod, he cursed and said, "There're some safety pins in the bathroom. Why don't you go in there and do some repairs?"

When she emerged a few minutes later, he seemed to be waiting for her, still standing in the place she'd left him.

"What about dinner?" she asked abruptly, hoping to deflect his attention. She plucked an Eddie Duchin album from the rack and studied the cover too intently. "Aren't you going to open a couple of cans?"

"That, my lady, is a sexist remark if I ever heard one." He closed the gap between them with a single stride.

"I'm sorry, but I'm starving and you promised me dinner."

"You said you weren't hungry."

"I was only being polite."

"I see." His lazy smile deepened the grooves at the corners of his mouth.

"Can we play this one?" She thrust the album at him, when his probing eyes told her his next move wouldn't be toward the kitchen.

"You like Duchin?" He slid the record carefully out of its sleeve.

"Yes. Well, I only know what I heard in the movie about his life."

"You're in for a treat, then. Kick off your shoes and relax on the couch, while I get busy."

"Can't I help?"

"No one comes in the kitchen while I cook."

"Now you sound like Barney." She smiled. "Afraid I'll learn your secrets?"

His eyes twinkled. "Nope. Afraid I'll never get as far as boiling water if you're with me. You have a terribly unsettling effect on me, in case you haven't noticed."

Was he joking or was he giving her fair warning? Either way, it was enough to prevent her from insisting further.

He was a purposeful man who kept things handy only if they served a need. The bicycle on the wall, for instance, ready and waiting. As long as Addie was here, he might decide to make use of her, too. He'd kiss her until she couldn't remember her name, then set her aside. No concern of his, the flotsam of emotions he left behind.

Or was he like that?

As it happened, contrived compliments on his culinary skills were unnecessary. Dinner was a work of art— boned and lightly breaded chicken breasts with an unusual fruit sauce, browned new potatoes, and a salad made from a bit of everything.

"That was wonderful," she said truthfully, as they were having coffee. "I'd recommend this restaurant to anyone."

"It's an exclusive establishment. I screen my patrons carefully." Reaching across the table, he brushed his thumb lightly over her knuckles, triggering a shuddering response all out of proportion to his touch.

Only female guests? she wondered, thinking again of what Kevin had hinted about Thorne's prowess with women. Hence the huge couch, wide enough to accommodate two? Was his insistence on living away from the main house as much to ensure privacy as to retain a measure of independence?

"My specialty is chicken and dumplings," she said quickly. "I'll have to make it for you sometime." Did that sound as if she was wheedling a return visit? Probably.

"It's a date." He reached out again to capture her hand, turning the palm up for closer scrutiny.

"It's Barney's favorite meal," she went on. "I do the dumplings a different way from most. I make two small loaves and slice them for serving."

Was he listening?

A hand was only a hand. She had no reason to feel threatened by the attention he was giving hers. "You read palms?" she teased, making light of her discomfort.

His lower lip jutted out delectably, and one brow furrowed in exaggerated concentration. "Hmm. Interesting."

"What?"

"The skin is baby soft. Yet the tips of the fingers are callused. You must play the guitar."

"Barney taught me," she said, impressed with his detective work. "He learned when he was in the navy."

"That means you sing."

"It means I *try*."

"I'd like to hear you."

She grimaced and drew her hand away. "Fat chance of that."

"What kind of songs do you play? Pop? Country?"

"Folk ballads mostly. 'Barbara Allen.' 'Danny Boy.'"

"Barney's favorites," they said together, and laughed.

"I have a vivid image of this ever present grandfather of yours. The stereotypical gruff but lovable old codger of TV sitcoms."

"There's nothing stereotypical about Barney. He's one of a kind."

Thorne's eyes narrowed and he leaned back in his chair until it creaked. "Whoever tries to win your affections is going to have a big pair of shoes to fill. I wonder if anyone can."

She started to object to the evaluation, then changed her mind. Maybe she did use her grandfather as a measure of sorts. "Doesn't every girl have an ideal?" she asked lightly. "And what about you?" she went on. "You're a music lover. Didn't you ever take up an instrument just for fun?"

"I played the sax in college."

"And?"

He grinned. "The tenants in my apartment building started up a petition against me."

"Really?"

"Not exactly. But they gave me scathing looks whenever I met them in the elevator."

She smiled, then seeing a chance, however slim, to introduce a subject that had been gnawing at her, took it. "Did you meet your wife while you were in college?"

His face didn't change. Only a slight pause indicated that he felt she might be prying. "No. After graduation, when I was working for the law firm that handled her father's accounts. It was Jan who convinced me to accept George's offer to work for Mandeville."

That wasn't the way Kevin had told it. "I would have thought you'd do that, anyway, close as the two of you were."

"I felt he'd done too much for me already. Maybe I wanted to prove something. I don't really remember. Anyway, Jan pushed, and I'm glad she did, even though things didn't work out entirely as planned."

"You found it confining working exclusively for one company?"

"With Mandeville's diversification? Not at all. I meant . . . something else entirely." He frowned.

"I'm sorry," she said quickly. "You've been slaving over a hot stove. We shouldn't talk business tonight."

But had they been talking about business? Or was he thinking of Jan and their failed marriage? Now she wished she hadn't said anything.

One of his index fingers traced the rim of his coffee cup as he regarded her. He might have been stroking her skin for the sensation the movement caused. If thoughts of his ex-wife had awakened in him a need to compensate for his loss, it was time for defensive action.

She got up and began stacking the dishes. "Now it's your turn to relax while I work."

"Let it wait."

"Barney and I have a rule. Whoever does the cooking doesn't do the dishes."

"Barney isn't here." His brow creased in a small frown. "Or is he?"

She decided to ignore the implication. "Fair's fair, according to anybody's rules."

Reluctantly he stood up, too, and crossed to the stereo again. "I'll put on another record. What would you like?"

"Oh, whatever you want."

His distance gave her the chance to follow through with what she'd begun. Picking up the dishes she'd stacked, she made her way to the kitchen. Maybe the clatter and clink, the swoosh and splash, would disarm the ticking bomb of her feelings for him. "At least I can scrape and rinse and . . ." she began.

Her voice faltered as she pushed through the swinging half-door and saw the clutter. Dishes, spoons, bowls and pots were everywhere. A spill of flour had been tracked across the floor and a trash basket was overturned. It looked as if Thorne had cooked a banquet for fifty, not two.

He leaned against the doorjamb and grinned. "Things tend to get out of control when I cook."

"To put it mildly."

"Forget it. I have a dishwasher."

"Washing dishes would be only the first step in . . ."

"A long climb to the top of Mount Everest?" he finished for her.

"Something like that."

"Addie," he coaxed, holding out one hand to her. "Let's not be domestic tonight. Harry James is on the turntable."

She didn't particularly like Harry James. His trumpet always got in the way of the melody. But she suspected saying *that* to Thorne would have been heresy.

"We can listen as we work."

With a groan of frustration, he caught the towel she was preparing to tie around her middle for an apron. She held it fast and they struggled over it briefly, moving closer and closer until she thudded against him.

She tried for a playful laugh, but it didn't work. He wasn't laughing. Her breath caught in her throat.

"Maybe I'd better take you home," he said.

"Maybe," she managed.

She felt one of his hands at the small of her back, the other between her shoulder blades. They pressed her closer still, guiding her into an inevitable kiss.

Closing her eyes and lifting her mouth to his, she set her consciousness free. What was the use? was her last clear thought, before he ground his scorching lips into hers as though addicted to the sweetness he remembered there.

Magic shimmered in that kiss. It was music and poetry, and unreasoning delight. It was fire and ice, and it was breathtaking. All suspicion between them seemed suddenly obliterated. It was a kiss that would never be matched.

But it was. By the one that followed, and the one after that. Now her arms were around him, allowing her to lay a claim of her own to the strength and breadth of his shoulders, where the heated moisture of his skin was evident through his shirt.

Up, up, moved her questing fingers, along the thickness of his neck, to the crispness of his hair. The sensations struck new chords of pleasure. Pleasure. She was weighted to the toes with it.

"Those lips," he muttered, taking them twice again before he went on, "I can't stay away from them."

For the first time, she became aware of the music. If it was Harry James, she'd misjudged him. The trumpet was plaintive and beautiful, speaking a wonderful language she understood for the first time. The drum. Was it the drum? Its pulsating rhythm seemed to echo the inner rhythm of Thorne's body and hers.

"How is it possible?" he whispered against her hair.

"How is what possible?"

"You don't fuss with your hair, your makeup, your clothes. Anything. Yet you always look like an angel."

How is it possible? she wanted to repeat, asking the same question of him.

"I'd better take you home while I still can." With each word his heated breath sent a delicious message to her ear, filling her with a joy that was almost painful in its intensity.

"You said that before." Their roles had reversed. Should she be the one asking to be taken home? "Besides, it's only a few steps. I think I could manage it from here without an escort."

With mock ferocity, he caught a fist of her hair and pulled it back to study her face. "Do you have an argument for everything?"

"Isn't argument a law of logic?"

"What does either of us know about logic?" Sweeping her off her feet, he backed into the living room, dim now in contrast with the brightly lit kitchen.

"I thought we were leaving," she protested, as he placed her on the couch and then lay beside her.

"We are." He dipped his head to press his mouth to the side of her neck. "Eventually."

She closed her eyes. No doubt the imprint of his lips would still be there later, when she studied herself in the mirror....

"I wonder," he murmured. "Is there a square inch of you that isn't flawless?"

Before she answered, as if she could, his lips began to skim down the heated surface of her neck in merciless slow motion, to settle at the hollow of her throat, to bathe it with the warmth of his mouth and caress it with the moistness of his tongue.

"What am I going to do about you?" he muttered, as if each syllable had to be forced out into the open. "God knows, I've tried, but I can't keep my hands off you. In the face of everything that's happened between us, I can't stop kissing you, wanting you. I've never felt so out of control."

Control. In the face of everything that had happened? His question struck a raucous chord. For a few moments it only hung there without registering. Then it did. *What am I going to do about you?*

He was trying with all his being *not* to care for her. She might have been a terrible illness he was trying desperately to cure. The magnitude of the insult shattered everything she'd been feeling, and fury took over.

"There's a simple solution," she said tightly.

Catching the change in her at once, he shrank back to look at her. The blue velvet of his eyes became a smoky gray.

"What solution?"

"You're agonizing over how to get rid of me? Don't bother about it. I'll be going back to California soon."

"If only it were that simple."

"It *is* that simple. When I was a little girl I hated spinach—"

"Another story with a moral?" He groaned. "Now?"

"I hated spinach," she went on. "Mother had the idea it contained nutrients found in nothing else, so we had it once a week, like it or not."

"Maybe she'd seen too many Popeye cartoons."

"Barney told me not to think about the taste. To think, instead, about all those minerals rushing to every part of my body. Those frisky little vitamins darting around inside me, making my hair shiny and my eyes bright."

He raised an eyebrow. "Then I have spinach to thank for those eyes, that hair—"

"It's the same thing in reverse," she went on, not intending to be sidetracked by a mouthful of blarney. "Don't think of me the way I am when we're together, or your lust for me. Think of the mercenary, money-hungry, grasping package I am inside, and it should be a snap for you to turn away."

"I never said you were those things." He put his fingers to her cheek.

She brushed his hand away. "Didn't you?"

"It's a fact of life. The scramble for money makes good people do strange things. Mother turns on daughter. Father and son come to blows. A friend of mine is working on a case that makes me physically ill. An elderly man who spent the last fifteen years of his life alone died leaving his money to a handful of his favorite charities. Now the relatives have come out of the woodwork in droves, bent on trying to break his will."

Suddenly she felt very foolish, very vulnerable. She struggled to sit up and straighten her clothing.

With maddening self-assurance, he stood up and stretched. "We'll talk about it tomorrow, when you've cooled off."

"I won't be going on any more excursions."

"Oh?" His good humor seemed to slip a notch.

"I've seen all of Boston I care to see."

"Meaning you've seen all you care to see of me."

"Meaning I'm not writing a book about Boston for the armchair traveler. I want to spend the rest of my stay with my aunt."

"Your aunt," he repeated, his voice flat and ugly.

"Miriam told me to call her 'aunt.' I can't very well say 'my great-great-great-grandfather's nephew's granddaughter,' every time I refer to her, can I?"

He caught her arm as she started past him, painfully at first, then he seemed to think better of it and opened and closed his fingers tentatively. "One-fourth of the people on this planet are related to us in one way or another if you dig deeply enough."

"I won't argue with you." She looked pointedly at the hand that detained her.

"That'll be a novelty." As he spat out the words, not a trace of the Sir Galahad charm he'd used on her all evening remained.

"I'd like to use the bathroom before I go."

Releasing her, he made a Shakespearean actor's sweeping gesture toward the hallway.

She could still feel the heat of his outrage as she combed her hair and splashed water on her face, wondering if Thorne was standing outside the door waiting to pounce on her with some new accusation when she emerged.

He wasn't. He was across the room on the telephone, with his back to her. He was shuffling through some papers and arguing about a court date that had been moved to an inconvenient time.

"I can't drop everything and fly up there without notice. I've appointments to arrange. People to put off."

She was in luck. Her coat and handbag were nearby. She was able to retrieve them and slip out without being seen.

As she stepped outside, a malicious gust of wind struck her full in the face, making her eyes smart and lifting her hair, undoing all she'd done with her comb. Or was it the wind that stung her eyes?

With her head erect and her shoulders squared, she placed one foot in front of the other. There was no need to hurry. Thorne wouldn't give chase. He was probably hoping the ground would swallow her up and solve his little problem for him.

CHAPTER TEN

"LET ME DO THAT for you." Unexpectedly, Kevin slid through the door that Addie hadn't realized was ajar, to help with the zipper of her sea-blue dress. He took a step back to study her, then made a circle of approval with his thumb and forefinger. "Spectacular. You should always wear—what do they call it—a halter neckline?"

"You don't think it's too...too..."

"Hell, no. Shoulders like yours were meant to be bared."

"Thank you."

Seeing him as he was now, wearing a dark dinner jacket and an innocent smile, his dark blond hair immaculately combed, she could almost believe she'd imagined what had gone on between them. Almost but not quite. He was only being complimentary to ensure her silence.

Still, Miriam cared for him. If he was willing to put aside their differences for the sake of appearances, she wouldn't make it difficult for him, as long as he stayed at arm's length.

"You look very dashing." At least that much was true.

"Think so?" He struck a jaunty pose and winked. "See you downstairs, luv. And, hey, give the competition hell."

What competition was that? Had he already been into the bottle?

After the things he'd said and done of late, she was certain the Madame Cassandra episode had been intentional, meant to drive a wedge between her and Thorne. Separate, to his way of thinking, they weren't as threatening.

When he'd ducked out of her room again, she surveyed herself in the mirror carefully, turning from side to side and looking over her shoulder. She couldn't shake the feeling Kevin might have done something to sabotage her appearance.

A Kick Me sign on her backside, for instance.

As guest of honor, she'd been kept out of the dining room during preparations, and so was as awed by the results of Miriam's work as anyone. A single long-stemmed rose, pink for the women, white for the men, had been placed at each setting, and the simple centerpiece of more pink and white roses appropriately matched the old-fashioned pattern of Miriam's favorite china. The rose-tinged water goblets added exactly the right touch of elegance to the table, along with the pale pink cards with each guest's name written in gold ink by someone with a fine hand.

On an impulse, guessing correctly that Miriam would have seated her next to Thorne, hence another uncomfortable evening, Addie dashed in at the first opportunity and moved the place cards hurriedly about. Her aunt would be somewhat dismayed at the rearranged seating, but could hardly fix it without appearing to play musical chairs.

In her haste to make the switches, Addie had placed a retired assemblyman on her left and Kevin on her right. The assemblyman, in the process of writing the story of his life, was determined to share slices of it, even if his audience was an unwilling one. At least his nonstop stories kept her from having to entertain her other dinner partner.

She'd set Thorne beside a stunning woman, whose white-blond hair was done in tiers of curls. In sharp contrast, the woman's eyebrows were black, and she wore a smoky gray, watered-silk dress that bared one shoulder. From her animated conversation and Thorne's frequent smiles, Addie gathered that neither of them minded the seating at all.

"Why is it Cameron always ends up with my ladies?" Kevin muttered under his breath.

"She's with you? She's lovely."

"She *was* with me. From the look of things, this party might effect not only your introduction to Boston society, but a reconciliation for the Camerons."

Addie infused a tone of idle curiosity into her voice. "She's Thorne's ex-wife?"

"Right. The glamorous Janice Allardyce Cameron." Kevin twisted his mouth to one side. "What I can't figure is why Miriam would have seated them together. She never did approve of Jan. Actually, I'm the one who invited her, and I can tell you Miriam wasn't pleased."

Addie's plate blurred. So that was what Kevin had meant about competition. He'd done it to her again, and he knew it. His admission that Miriam didn't approve of Thorne's ex-wife was proof that the woman's presence was designed to drive another wedge between Addie and Thorne. The knowledge that seeing the two together might cause Addie pain gave him further satisfaction. Probably he had no interest in Jan whatsoever.

"And you didn't have a reconciliation in mind when you brought her here, I suppose." She willed herself not to look in Thorne's direction.

"Why would I?" He donned an expression that would have convinced her if she hadn't fallen prey to it before.

"Everyone." Miriam's voice was high-pitched, as she tried to be heard over the hum of conversation. She clinked a spoon against her water glass and got to her feet.

Addie flexed her fingers for control, guessing what was in store for her.

Though introductions would have been more graceful had Miriam taken the guest of honor around the room to meet people one or two at a time, she'd evidently decided to take care of them all at once. After making an embarrassingly effusive speech, she asked her "beautiful newfound niece" to stand up, too, so that everyone could see her. If that wasn't bad enough, she asked for a round of applause.

Somehow Addie got through the meal, and if she was too quiet, Miriam would probably attribute it to shyness with strangers.

Afterward, when the guests were spilling through the house, dividing into groups for more intimate visiting, she was relieved to find herself at a safe distance from Thorne. He and his ex-wife made up a group of their own, if two could properly be called a group. Jan was entertaining him with a lively story, occasionally putting a hand on his shoulder to lean close and say something she apparently didn't want anyone else to hear. No one would have thought that, to look at them, there were problems in their relationship. Maybe there weren't—now. Maybe Kevin was right about their getting together again. Addie took a sip from the glass he had pressed on her, but it didn't alleviate the parched feeling at the back of her throat.

She turned her attention to Miriam, who was holding forth about Isaiah Rutherford and the things Addie had uncovered at the university library. "We were puzzled, Adeline and I," she said, "by several documents that proved he was in Boston, while others placed him in Rhode Island at the same time. Well, it seems there were two Isaiahs. One was a namesake."

From her experience with Barney, Addie recognized the glassy look people got in their eyes when forced to listen to stories about family trees. Trying to lead the conversation to a livelier topic, she mentioned the sights she'd seen since she arrived, and those she still hoped to see.

"Have you been to Salem?" someone asked.

"Not yet," Miriam answered for her. "But she's driving there on Monday with Thorne. It *is* Monday, isn't it?" she called. "Oh, Thorne!"

"I didn't hear you." He sauntered over to join them with Jan at his side, not giving Addie time for even a shivering breath in preparation.

"I was saying, you're taking Adeline to Salem on Monday."

"That's entirely up to Adeline." A frown creased his forehead. "She might have other plans."

"Other plans?" Miriam looked paler than usual, making the spots of rouge on her cheeks seem brighter. "Surely with your love of history, darling, you'll want to see Salem." She turned to Addie.

"She's welcome to make the drive with me," he said, directing his reply at Miriam, as if Addie weren't there. "But she'll have to make up her mind soon."

She has already made up her mind, Addie fumed silently.

"Thorne playing tourist guide?" Jan laughed merrily. "Miriam, you are the only person in the world who could force him to do anything so boring. Paul Revere and all that. No wonder he looks so tired. Poor baby."

"I don't think he's found it boring at all." Miriam pursed her lips. "He and Adeline have had some lovely times."

Jan looked from Miriam to Thorne and back to Miriam again in disbelief. "Would you really expect him to tell you the truth about it? I hope the ordeal has been worth it. Are you enjoying yourself, Adeline?"

"Very much," Addie managed.

Never given to snap judgments, she wasn't comfortable with her unreasoning dislike of the woman. It could only have been jealousy, and that was ridiculous. Even if Thorne and Jan had discovered each other again, it had nothing to do with her.

"You have to remember," Kevin broke in, "Addie's from California. There isn't much history out there. Just movie stars. She's probably grown up thinking our country began on the back lot of Universal Studios."

"So poor Thorne was elected teacher. I'm not sure he'll survive."

"Have you ever been to California, Jan?" Addie asked, hoping to change the subject smoothly.

"Once." The woman wrinkled her nose. "And once was enough. The smog, the inedible food, even in the finest restaurants. And the houses. All so squat and ugly. Pink, yellow, aquamarine. Like stucco Easter eggs."

"There are a few million people who don't agree with you," Thorne drawled. "Los Angeles isn't exactly a ghost town."

"Perhaps they're hooked on beaches. As far as I'm concerned, the ocean is California's only excuse for

being. Don't you ever go to the beach, Addie?" Jan
arched one carefully penciled eyebrow. "I'm curious
about a California girl who doesn't sport a golden tan."

"She has delicate skin," Miriam ventured timidly. "It
likely burns painfully if it's exposed to the sun for long.
It's always been so with me."

"I wouldn't change a thing about her." Kevin got up
to refill the wineglass he'd carried from the dinner table.
"In that greeny blue dress she looks as enticing as a little
mermaid."

Jan lay a hand on Thorne's shoulder and smiled at
him, before turning back to Kevin. "Why don't you tell
us what a mermaid looks like, dear? I don't doubt that
you've seen your share of them in the bottom of a glass."

He tasted his drink. "Oh . . . like Addie, I'd say. Up-
tilted amber eyes, flowing brown hair, touched with
golden lights, clear pale skin, fresh from a morning
plunge in the sea."

"You're making her sound like that enchantress,
Circe," Jan said, her voice colored with exaggerated
drama. "She had the power to turn men into wild
beasts."

Kevin snapped his fingers. "That's Addie, all right."

It was an embarrassing exchange, seemingly borne of
some desire in Jan to humiliate her. Had she and Kevin
discussed Addie's intrusion into the family on their way
to the party earlier? Had Addie been the brunt of the
woman's stories earlier—the ones that had made Thorne
laugh? The thought was sobering.

Or was there nothing personal in it? Was Jan one of
those people who felt anyone was fair game for her sarcasm?

In any case, Addie was relieved when the assembly-man who'd been her dinner partner saw an opening for one of his lengthy tales and pounced on it.

When he took a breath, Jan began to ease herself gracefully away from the group. "Thorne!" She wiggled her fingers to summon him. "There's someone I want you to meet."

He nodded, then turned back to Addie. "Let me know," he said quietly.

Kevin favored Addie with a lazy smile. "I think somebody has stolen my date. Care to take a stroll to burn off the extra calories?"

"At this time of night?" Looking perturbed, Miriam knotted and unknotted her lacy handkerchief.

"I meant in the garden," he said. "I doubt we'd come across any muggers out there."

Miriam reached out to close a hand over his. "Be a dear boy and get me a glass of white wine, will you?"

"Another, Auntie?" he teased. "Are you sure you should? I wouldn't want you to start dancing on the table with a lamp shade on your head."

"I'll leave such shenanigans to you," she said, slapping his shoulder playfully. When he'd gone, her smile faded and she turned to Addie. "You've been spending time with Kevin, I've noticed."

"Well..."

"I'd be less than honest if I didn't warn you that he can be a scamp and needs a good scolding now and then." Miriam smoothed the neckline of her pink lace dress, appearing to take great care in choosing her words. "If you know what I mean."

Addie knew. She knew, too, that Miriam was distressed about her matchmaking scheme coming apart at the seams. The woman scooted closer and looked in the direction Kevin had gone, as if to make sure no one could hear. "I need you to do something for me, dear."

"Anything."

"Allow Thorne to take you to Salem. It's important to get him away for the day."

Addie's heart turned over. Her glance moved to the place Thorne and Jan had been standing. They were gone. She swallowed hard. "Why should that be important to you?"

"It's because of Kevin." Miriam touched nervous fingers to her pearl necklace. "He's working on a business deal. It's one he might be able to bring to a successful conclusion if Thorne isn't around, as he says, 'breathing down his neck.'"

"Couldn't you simply ask Thorne to keep out of it?"

"Yes, but I'd like Kevin to believe, this once, that I have confidence in him. That I don't have Thorne standing by to bail him out in case of trouble. It might be just the thing to turn him around. It's what George would want. Will you help?"

"I've already refused Thorne's invitation, though he's pretending I haven't," Addie protested. "I know you think he and I have hit it off, but we haven't. We're simply too different. And no matter what people say, opposites don't attract."

There. She'd said it.

"It's your imagination."

"Is it also my imagination that he and Jan are getting along so well together?"

Miriam shook her head. "Getting along together at a social gathering is a far cry from getting back together. Thorne isn't twenty years old anymore. He's far too smart these days to jump back on the treadmill Jan built for him. And she's given up trying to coach him in his rise to power. Though I'll admit she seemed to be jealous of you tonight. She'd probably visualized him pining for her forever."

"Jealous of me? That's nonsense."

"Not at all. One only has to see how he looks at you to know he's beginning to care."

"Miriam!" Addie chided. "I really don't think my going to Salem with Thorne is a good idea." The woman wasn't above telling a white lie or two to get her way. Was the business deal another of those lies designed to help Cupid along?

"Just this once." Miriam's eyes were moist. "I promise not to press you again. As I said, Kevin can be a scamp, but I love him."

Addie sighed. It was impossible. Was she supposed to track Thorne and Jan down and interrupt whatever they were doing and ask him to take her to Salem after all?

"I'll arrange everything," Miriam promised, lowering her voice as Kevin returned with her wine. "Leave it to me."

As the minutes ticked by and became hours, people began leaving, and Addie began to hope. Maybe Miriam had thought of another way to solve her problem. Then she saw Thorne heading toward her, and knew she'd been indulging in wishful thinking.

"Miriam tells me you're going to honor me with your presence on Monday, after all." His shallow smile was derisive.

"If the invitation hasn't been withdrawn."

"From what I saw earlier, you've made up with Roper. Why not let him take you?"

She swallowed a tempting retort. All at once she was glad to be part of a scheme to get him out of town. It would serve him right.

Or was she only inventing excuses to do what she wanted to do anyway? It had been torture being in the same room with him tonight, wondering how he felt about her after their quarrel, watching him with Jan. Was she hoping that the trip might be her last chance to erase the ugliness between them and try for a fresh start? Or did she simply want to have the memory of one more day with him to take back to Los Angeles?

"I thought as long as you were going anyway, it wouldn't make much sense to take Kevin away from business, as well," she said.

"He wouldn't mind. He'd rather do anything than tend to his job." Nothing in his voice suggested that Addie had been right about his feelings for her. When he left her side this evening, he'd probably go and cry on Jan's shoulder.

"If you don't want me along," she threw at him, "just say so."

For a moment, she thought he would. "Monday. Eight o'clock." The calm in his voice sounded somehow ominous. "We'll want an early start."

Speak for yourself, she muttered silently.

CHAPTER ELEVEN

MONDAY MORNING was gray and sullen, with a bite in the air, as a reminder that winter had not entirely given way to spring. After crossing the bridge, Thorne and Addie drove north on Route 1.

The on-again, off-again truce was on at the moment, and while there wasn't the closeness between them that they'd experienced for a time, there wasn't bitterness, either. They actually managed to reach Salem without a single verbal attack or snide remark.

The Witch House and the Witch Museum were first on the agenda. Thorne had been right. There was much more to see in this beautiful little town than the things associated with the hideous seventeenth-century witch hunts. They lingered over an early lunch and spent the afternoon wandering about until streaks of lightning in the distance, crackling thunder and a darkening sky sent them on their way.

Storms had always frightened Addie, and this one promised to be especially violent. The rain was coming down in blinding sheets by the time they neared Amesbury. Thorne spoke with exaggerated calm, trying to make her believe that the storm was nothing to worry about. But he leaned into the wheel and clutched it with great concentration. Finally he had to admit defeat.

"There's an inn up the road." He squinted through the blackness. "I'll get you settled. You might as well be comfortable until it clears."

"And if it doesn't clear?"

"I'll take a second room. We'll spend the night."

Addie didn't argue. She couldn't remember ever seeing such lightning. The blinding flashes of eerie brightness that illuminated the countryside were more like fireworks on the Fourth of July.

The inn, a converted eighteenth-century mansion, was probably charming. But she was in no state to be charmed. Even tucked into the snug room that would be hers, at least for a few hours, she felt like the heroine in an old horror movie, waiting for the monster to make his move.

"The lightning isn't as close as it seems," Thorne assured her.

"It couldn't be, or we'd be toast," she said, shivering in one of the wing chairs, a pillow clutched to her chin.

"Try to get some rest while I'm gone." He picked up his briefcase.

She was on her feet. "You aren't going out again?"

His face mirrored his indecision. "It'd be a shame to come this far and not get these papers signed."

"The weather might clear."

"It isn't likely." He looked tentatively at the door, then back at Addie. "Do you want me to stay?"

She didn't want to say it. If he stayed, she didn't want it to be on her account. "The roads are probably flooded. You wouldn't get far."

"Do *you* want me to stay?"

"Yes." She winced as the lamp flickered in response to a roll of thunder. "It doesn't rain like this in California."

"Do you work for the Chamber of Commerce?" He laughed. "It rains so hard there that trees slide down hillsides, and houses wash into the ocean."

"You've been reading the newspapers." She smiled weakly.

"And the accounts are highly exaggerated?"

"Maybe not. But we don't have lightning. At least—" she shivered involuntarily "—not like this."

He set his briefcase down. "Let me help you," he offered, coming over to slip the coat from her shoulders. He pressed firm hands to her upper back, circling them slowly.

"Mmm. That feels good." She allowed her head to fall to one side and then the other as he worked. "Give me a minute to remind myself that rain gives us spring flowers—and rainbows."

"Not to mention the pots of gold at the ends of said rainbows," he added, using his knuckles on a place between her shoulder blades.

"The atmosphere in haunted mansion movies."

"And my favorite dance number in my favorite musical, *Singin' in the Rain*."

It was Addie's favorite musical, too. Warmed by new enthusiasm, she looked up at him. "Thank you, Thorne. I'm fine now."

"You're sure? Then I'll go downstairs and—"

"No." Instinctively she caught his hand, realizing in that brief moment that her fear wasn't due entirely to the storm. It was more. Much more. This might well be the only night they would ever have together. She didn't want to squander a precious second of it.

"I have to make arrangements for another room."

"It isn't necessary. There are twin beds if we want to rest. We're only waiting out the storm."

"A lull in the weather, no matter how reassuring, won't necessarily mean the storm is over," he reminded her, looking toward the window. "We might as well accept the fact that we're stuck for the night."

Stuck. Was that how he felt? "I'd rather not be alone. Please. I won't be getting much sleep, anyway, especially if you're right and the worst of the storm isn't over yet."

He nudged the fringed edge of the shag rug with his toe. "I doubt I would, either. With you lying only a couple of feet away."

"Oh, I won't disturb you," she promised, her thoughts too erratic at the moment to grasp his meaning.

"Wanna bet?" His blue eyes crinkled mischievously.

But it was decided. A second room would only be troublesome and expensive, as well as lonely. While Thorne made a call to the client who was expecting him, Addie took a hasty shower, hoping to get in and out before the lightning struck again in earnest.

She emerged from the bathroom scrub-faced, freshly shampooed and wrapped snugly in one of the oversize terry cloth robes provided by the management. Thorne had ordered a bottle of wine, as well as bowls of steaming clam chowder, fresh crusty bread and an assortment of cheeses from room service. The young man who'd shown them to their room earlier had set a crackling fire in the fireplace.

"I wasn't able to get through to Miriam." His eyes swept over her appreciatively as if she'd been wearing a diaphanous nightgown, instead of the bulky cover-up that was anything but provocative. "There's trouble with the phone lines. They're going to call back."

"Good. I wouldn't want her to worry." Addie had a notion, though, that the older woman wouldn't do much worrying when she knew Addie was with Thorne. She'd probably dance with glee, looking on their forced night together as part of Cupid's plan.

Thorne took his turn in the bathroom and emerged a few minutes later dressed, like her, in one of the inn's bathrobes. Seated beside him on enormous floor cushions in the flickering orange glow of the fire, Addie felt close to him all over again. And safe. As if he, like a superhero in the comics, could thrust out a hand and divert the most malicious of lightning bolts. As she looked at him, she realized why his gaze had been so approving. There was something incredibly sexy about the ill-fitting wrap and the freshly shaved man at her elbow.

"You never talk about your family," she said absently, sipping the wine.

"I have a mother, a father and two brothers."

The mental picture was staggering. Were the other two Cameron boys as attractive as this one? "Older or younger?" she asked.

"Younger."

There were so many other things she wanted to know about him, but where did she start? He wasn't an easy man to draw out. "What is it they say about the oldest child?"

"I wouldn't know." He stared at the fire.

"He's driven to higher achievements." She waited, but he added nothing. The odd feeling came to her that he was drawing away. "Cameron is Scottish, of course," she went on. "And you look Scottish."

"What does a Scotsman look like?"

"Oh, he has a stubborn jaw and blue eyes that turn steely gray when he's angry."

"I see." He didn't look at her.

"What about your mother's side of the family? Have you ever traced your family tree?"

He set his glass down harder than necessary. "I could be descended from Ghengis Khan or Tarzan, and I wouldn't be any different for it. I am what I am."

"Like it or not, we're all made up of our inherited traits. While environment is terribly important, too, recent studies show—"

"I don't give a damn for your recent studies. Tell me, if you'd found a close-fisted miser or a raving psychopath in your closet, instead of a generous warmhearted woman like Miriam, would you be so fired up about roots and bloodlines?"

"I—I don't know." He was doing it again. He was actually angry. But why? She returned his furious glare with one better. "I was only making conversation."

"I'm sorry." He glared toward the window, as if the two words he'd uttered were painful ones.

It was the most insincere apology she'd ever received. "No," she shot back. "*I'm* sorry. I keep forgetting how impossible you are. How impossible we are together."

"I was wrong to jump on you," he said, calm now that she was getting excited.

"Yes, you were! This time, and the last time, and the time before that. You remind me of a character in an old Abbott and Costello movie."

"I do?" One eyebrow peaked.

"This character, a huge strongman type, is very gentle and well-behaved, until Costello says a certain word that sets him off. Then he goes berserk and pummels Costello with his fists. He apologizes afterward, but poor Costello keeps forgetting. He says the word again and the man pummels him again. It's terribly funny in the movie. But it isn't very funny in real life."

"The word was 'pokomoko.'" Thorne grinned foolishly. "I remember the movie."

When he tried to touch her arm, she got to her knees. "Why did you bring me here if you hate me so much?"

Surprise flickered across his face. "I don't hate you, Addie. On the contrary—"

"I shudder to think of how you'd behave if you did." She stood up quickly and moved into the shadows, not wanting to give him the satisfaction of seeing that she was hurt. "The wine made me sleepy. I'm going to bed."

"It's only nine o'clock. Besides, you didn't have that much."

"I had enough. And not only of the wine." She vehemently threw back one of the quilted bedspreads. "This one, away from the window, will be mine. If you have no objections.

"Even if you *have*," she muttered to herself.

"I didn't mean to hurt you." He got up, too, and followed her, to sit beside her as she slid between the sheets and turned her back on him. "It was inexcusable."

"Go away."

"I'm sorry. Not only for tonight, but for the other nights I've said things to hurt you. Ugly things I knew were untrue when I was saying them. With only circumstantial evidence I've been blaming you for faults I've found in others. And maybe unconsciously, I envy you and Barney. My family was never close. My folks split up when I was six. Both of them remarried and had other children. I didn't feel as if I belonged anywhere."

When her only response was a grunt, he went on, his hand resting on her arm, his fingers crawling up to caress her skin under the wide sleeves of the robe. "I was encouraged by both sides to strike out on my own as soon as I was able, and so I did."

"You don't have to tell me all this," she said, turning to look at him.

"But I do. After I left home, I found a job in the ship-
ping room at Mandeville Chocolates. Something went
wrong with an order. There was trouble that resulted in
the company losing an important account. I was called on
the carpet by the big boss, George. Pretty cocky in those
days, mad at the world for the hand I'd been dealt and
feeling that I'd been selected as scapegoat because I was
young, I told him in the most colorful language I could
muster what he could do with his job."

"How did he take it?"

"He laughed, then invited me home to meet his wife.
She'd appreciate an employee who wasn't a yes-man, he
said."

Addie watched him intently as he went on, describing
all the things George and Miriam had done for him, not
only taking him into their home and making his educa-
tion possible, but treating him as if he were their own son.

His long lashes were sooty against his cheeks when he
looked down. His blue eyes were dark and intense when
he didn't. Addie's resentment dwindled to nothing.

He and Jan had married too young. Her childhood
had been as lonely as his. Her parents traveled most of
the time and left her in the care of servants. This gave
them something in common. But the marriage was wrong
from the start. Each expected the marriage to be a cure-
all for life's problems. It wasn't. It only created new ones.

"It was good seeing each other at the party. The bitterness is over. We can laugh at what had once seemed to
be a tragedy. Best of all, we can even be friends—as long
as we aren't married to each other."

Friends. Only friends.

So, unintentionally, Kevin had done Thorne a favor.
"Do you ever see your family?" she asked, wanting to

hug herself in exhilaration. Better still, wanting to hug Thorne.

"We correspond at regular intervals and exchange greeting cards at the appropriate times. I make it a point to fly out and spend a strained and rather tedious Thanksgiving with my mother one year, and my father the next." Thorne cleared his throat, likely feeling that he'd revealed too much of himself. "Enough of that. Now let's hear about you."

"What do you want to know?" She had no secrets. There was no part of her he wasn't welcome to examine and cross-examine.

"Everything. Not just those little fables you invent to put me in my place. Abbott and Costello. Popeye. Barney and your first Thanksgiving dinner. I want to know everything about the person you are." He shifted his position, stretching out so that his elbow rested on the bed, his head rested on the heel of his hand, and they were face-to-face. "We'll start with a question."

"I'm ready."

"Why did you come with me today?"

Ouch. The question jolted her from the flower-strewn path her thoughts had been taking as she dissected his face mentally, feature by feature, then allowed those features to return again to the stirring and sensual whole.

It was a question that begged for an answer that was not a lie, perhaps, but a half-truth. How could she tell him she'd come with him to give Kevin a chance to accomplish something on his own? It would be Abbott and Costello and pokomoko all over again. And it wouldn't have been the true reason, anyway. It would only have been the excuse she'd given herself.

But was she prepared to declare herself yet?

"I wanted to see Salem," she said. Not accustomed to such evasiveness, she felt as if her heart were tapping out a message in Morse code. One Thorne could hear and decipher. Not true. Not true. Not true.

"You made it clear that you didn't want to go anywhere with me again. What changed your mind?"

"I—I wanted to be with you," she said thickly, seeing no other choice.

His eyes met hers and darkened. "That was exactly the answer I wanted."

"Do I get points for it?" she asked, embarrassed by her admission, when he'd admitted nothing.

"Enough of that." His growl of exasperation was half in earnest. "We've wasted too much time already."

"We?"

"You don't expect me to take all the blame, do you?" His hand moved to her neck to rearrange the bunched-up thickness of her robe's shawl collar. As his index finger, warm and faintly rough, touched her neck, she was overcome with an unfamiliar and unexpected sensation. A sensation so powerful her eyes closed with the weight of it.

Closing your eyes is an invitation to be kissed, a small voice said, intruding on her joy. *Yes, yes, yes,* she answered.

The kiss began hesitantly with the mingling of breath with breath. Then her lips opened, as his did. Her head turned, too, as his did, in unison, to allow a perfect meeting. A meeting that pulled them together into a warm swirling darkness of discovery.

It was a technicolor kiss. With stereophonic sound and cinemascope, all the better for their having kissed before and for the certainty that they would kiss again. And again. As a young girl dreaming about love, she'd wondered if, when the newness wore off, the thrill of that first kiss would remain. Now her heart could answer.

"It *has* been my fault," he admitted huskily, his wonderful mouth seeking the pulse at the base of her throat. "I couldn't get past the people I've known. The experiences I've had with users. With people who pretend to care for each other when they only want to exploit them."

"Shh." Addie touched a finger to his lips and raised her head to replace the touch with a kiss.

"I'll make it up to you."

"You already have," she answered.

"When you agreed to come with me, you knew this would happen, didn't you?"

"Didn't *you?*"

His robe was still fastened around his waist with the sash, but it wasn't wrapped as tightly as her own. The expanse of his broad chest with its stirring mat of dark hair held her transfixed and sent her imagination bursting through its bonds.

With a shuddering sigh, he eased her robe open, unwrapping her as he would have unwrapped a special treasured gift.

"Oh, Addie." His voice was nearly inaudible. "There's so much I have to say to you. So much to explain."

"Now?" she teased.

"Later," he agreed. "Now I only want to make love to you."

She tensed, readying herself. But the bedside phone rang, a shrill ugly ring that demanded immediate attention.

It rang again.

At first she hoped Thorne wouldn't answer. The phone was an alien being invading her private world.

"It could be Miriam," he said, at the same time she thought of it.

Sitting up, he squared his shoulders before reaching for the receiver, and then ran his fingers through the delicious black tumble of his hair, as if the person on the other end of the line would see the disorder and guess what they'd been doing.

Addie giggled at the thought. The caller might also have been Thorne's client, or merely the operator saying the lines were still down. It didn't matter. She didn't listen to the conversation, only to the sound the words made as they rumbled through Thorne's chest.

On and on the conversation went before she realized that if it was Miriam, she might ask to speak to her. Addie didn't want to sound intoxicated when she took the receiver, as she probably would if she didn't regain control of herself.

She needn't have worried. He hung up without asking if she wanted to say something. He didn't even look at her as he rose abruptly, gave his sash a furious yank and stalked across the room to stare out the window.

Bad news certainly. Had his client decided to back out of their contract? Was the world coming to an end—or just *her* world?

When he turned toward her again, his face had changed. And it was a change that chilled her.

"I'm going to ask you again." His lips took a mocking twist. "Why did you come with me today?"

"I've already told you." She answered haltingly, wondering what he'd heard on the phone that could have triggered the transformation.

"You told me. But this time I want the truth."

The truth. Addie wasn't even sure she knew truth anymore. The rain had slowed to a gentle patter, tapping the windowpanes and obscuring the night sky.

The resounding joy of discovery inside her dwindled to an icy hush. "You act as if you already know what you consider to be the truth."

"That was Mack Garner, the head of accounting at Mandeville and a longtime friend of mine. You didn't know all big expenditures had to be cleared with me, did you? Roper evidently forgot that, too."

"What are you talking about?" She brushed her hair back with the heel of her hand. Her forehead was moist, though the room was chill now with the dying fire. Her golden eyes widened as she tried to recall exactly what Miriam had said. Kevin was trying to put through a business deal. He didn't want Thorne in the way.

"Why did you come with me?" he asked again, menace in the calm repetition and his slow stealthy approach. "Shall I answer for you?"

"It's true I wanted to see Salem," she began, after a thoughtful pause that allowed her to adjust to the new tension the ups and downs of their relationship brought with it. "But that wasn't the only—"

"Roper wanted me out of the city. After dinner on Friday, the two of you had your heads together for most of the evening. That's when you set it up. Something he wanted, for something you wanted."

"That's not true." She hadn't thought he'd even noticed Kevin sitting with her. He'd been too intent on entertaining and being entertained by his ex-wife.

"Two old friends," he snarled. "Or should I say, co-conspirators?"

"That's enough." She sat up, pressing her back against the padded headboard to put as much distance between them as possible. "It wasn't Kevin who asked me to go with you. It was Miriam."

"I blame myself," he went on, not listening. He slapped a hand against his thigh so hard it made Addie wince. "If I hadn't been walking an emotional tightrope myself lately, spinning in all directions at once, I'd have suspected something when he agreed to attend one of Miriam's dinner parties. It's totally out of character."

An emotional tightrope. Another shot at Addie.

"You said, 'Something he wanted, for something I wanted.' Exactly what did you mean by that?" she asked.

"Planning to play innocent all the way, are you?" He sneered. "Okay. Roper would convince Miriam to sign over some securities to your grandfather to ensure his loan, *if* you got me out of the way long enough for him to put through a deal I've been opposing. A deal that looks good on paper, but carries far too great a risk."

"Barney would never accept that kind of help," Addie protested. "He's too proud."

"He would if he didn't know about it until it was all over. If Miriam made an agreement with the bank not to mention the reason for their change of heart."

He sounded so confident. It had to be true. "I didn't know."

"Considering your feelings for your grandfather, do you expect me to believe that? Mack said Roper was fairly crowing about putting one over on me, now that he had Miriam's little niece on his side. If things work out, he said he might even give you a bonus."

"If Kevin said that, it isn't true."

"True? Where does truth fit into your neat little plan?"

"I suppose I planned the rain," she murmured, thrusting the ghosts of pleasure away to make room for reality.

He didn't speak for a long moment. "I wouldn't be surprised to hear that you could. Circe, Jan called you. The irresistible siren who had the power to lure men to destruction."

"Oh, yes, Circe," she hurled back at him. "Another in a long line of female characters invented by men to excuse their own weaknesses."

One of his eyes narrowed. "Good point. I walked right into the trap with my eyes open."

She almost questioned him about what he meant by "trap," but decided against it. What good would it do? The damage to her relationship with Thorne was irreparable. She couldn't blame Miriam, Kevin, or even herself. When she thought about it, their relationship had never stood a chance. Love wasn't love without trust, and trust had been the missing ingredient from the start.

Then why were his bitter feelings toward her so numbing? "Miriam isn't a fool," she said quietly, though her head was throbbing with the need to shout her innocence. "Isn't it possible she felt that confidence in Kevin this once was worth the risk?"

"You're right. Miriam isn't a fool," he admitted. "But her love of family is her weakness. As it didn't take *you* long to discover, even from a distance."

She almost leapt to her feet, wanting to confront him as near eye to eye as possible. But the shapeless garment she wore would have made her stance comedic. "So much concern about Miriam's money. It's terribly touching." Silently she ticked off the proper number of seconds to create a dramatic pause. "Almost *too* touching."

"What the hell is that supposed to mean?"

The storm was giving its all again. The rising wind threatened to shatter the window. Now and then lightning illuminated the room. Addie didn't care anymore. A far more fearsome storm was raging inside.

"It's obvious. You want to protect your investment in Miriam at all costs."

"My investment?"

"Yes. In time and effort. You're like an adopted son to her. Since she has no close relatives left, you expect to be her principal heir. Kevin told me so. It's why you despise him and always choose to believe the worst. He and I have a great deal in common."

Thorne seemed rooted to the spot. "He told you that, did he?"

"Yes. And as for your idea that I'm out for Miriam's money, I can only say that we tend to judge others' motives by our own."

He thrust out one hand. "You'd better not say anymore."

"It isn't fun being on the other end of an accusation, is it?"

A violent crash of thunder gratefully obliterated whatever insult he returned, and not wanting to hear it repeated, she lay down again and turned her back, hoping he'd take the hint.

She could hear him as he crossed to the window. Then there was nothing more for a very long time. At last she heard the creak of the springs as he sat down on the other bed.

Somehow the night passed. She didn't feel as if she'd slept. Her eyelids were thick and scratchy and she couldn't remember their ever closing. But they must have. It was light and Thorne was gone.

Her first thought was that he had left her. If he could have explained it to Miriam, he probably would have. But no. The curt note he'd propped against the lamp explained that he'd gone to his client's house to settle their business. Addie was to have breakfast downstairs before he returned. They wouldn't be stopping on their way back to Boston.

CHAPTER TWELVE

"I'M SORRY ABOUT THE STORM." Miriam dipped her spoon into her dish of chilled apricots, but didn't take any.

"We had time to explore Salem before it broke."

"I'm sorry I went behind your back, too." The admission was obviously painful for the older woman, who wasn't used to having to explain her actions to anyone. "You wouldn't have accepted the money from me directly. When Kevin suggested it, it seemed the only way."

"You only wanted to be kind. I'm sure Barney will understand that, and appreciate it. Everything will work out."

"I'm sure it will." Miriam dipped her spoon in the apricots again, with no more success. "I don't know what's keeping Thorne this morning."

"I imagine he had a million things to do at the office to make up for the time away," Addie said, deciding to play the game.

Miriam knew as well as she did that Thorne had no intention of taking any more meals at the table as long as Addie was here. He hadn't long to hold out. Her plane back to Los Angeles left early the next morning, and it couldn't be soon enough to suit her.

Though at the beginning she had enjoyed talking about Isaiah and the other Rutherfords, and going over old photographs, the enjoyment in it was gone. The morning dragged, and she was relieved when she was able to slip back to her room on the pretense of packing.

"Hey, I expected a few words of thanks for helping your dear old grandpa," Kevin said, breaking into her reverie.

Addie groaned. Would she never learn to close the door?

"Thank you," she said dully, deciding it was simpler than making accusations.

"Was Thorne furious?" He laughed. "Stupid-question department. Is Boston in Massachusetts?"

"Would you mind leaving me to my packing?" she asked, somehow suppressing the desire to slap the smug expression off his face.

He plucked a cigarette from a silver box on the table and lit it. "I warned you that you were betting on the wrong horse, honey. Cameron won't pocket a dime when Miriam shuffles off this mortal coil."

Money. The reference to Miriam's fortune again sent her thoughts reeling away from the indignity of their struggle. "You said that he hopes to inherit a great deal."

"Ah-ah. Don't misquote me." He looked at her through a cloud of rising smoke. "I said he has plans for Miriam's money. And preferably while Auntie is still around. Any money that falls into his hands will go to set up scholarships for deserving young law students. To finance hospital equipment for a proposed trauma center, one of George's pet projects. To set up law libraries, and God-only-knows-what-else—all in George's name. It's part of his obsession to make the man immortal."

His contempt building as he spoke, Kevin ground out his cigarette in a candy dish. "Can you imagine the stupidity of it? Spending a fortune to put the Mandeville name on a few brass plaques, instead of investing it in people?"

"Hospital equipment, scholarships, all those things you mentioned *are* people—or for people." Addie might have known it would be something like that. Thorne wasn't greedy. Why couldn't he see the same thing about her?

"Strangers, baby. Not family. You're family. I'm family. It isn't too late for us to join forces."

Addie crossed to the door and held it open. "Goodbye, Cousin Kevin," she said. "Don't bother to write."

"You aren't using your head." A corner of his mouth twisted in a sneer.

"You're right about that, at least," she muttered when he had gone.

Dinner was as strained as breakfast had been, with Miriam again pretending to wonder why Thorne hadn't joined them. "I'll have to call him," she said. "He's to take you to the airport."

"No need for that," Addie said quickly. "I plan to take a cab."

"But I want to ride along."

"So you will, Auntie," Kevin said sweetly. "I'll drive."

"This isn't like Thorne at all," Miriam insisted. "Could he have caught a bug in all that horrid weather?"

"I'd say something bit *him*." Kevin glanced at Addie meaningfully.

Miriam and her well-meant help, Boston, the house, the thought of Thorne's despising her, all of it threatened to suffocate her. She had to get off by herself, but slipping away again was difficult. Miriam wanted to spend every minute with her, and Kevin, unbelievably, was still making a pitch for a partnership.

He'd evidently brought his business deal to a successful conclusion when Addie had so thoughtfully "taken
Thorne out of his hair" and couldn't stop crowing about
it. Some months before, he had approached the hereto-
fore unapproachable owner of an ultraexpensive line of
"rejuvenating" cosmetics whose company George had
been after for years.

With brilliant diplomacy and unmatchable charm,
Kevin said, only half-kidding, he had reeled it all in under the Mandeville banner. He was bruised from all the
slaps on the back he'd been getting from executives who
hadn't known his name the week before.

"I bear no grudges," he said magnanimously. "Business is business. But I have a long memory."

When, hypnotized by his own words, he began out-
lining his strategy for Miriam, Addie saw her chance and
took it.

The stars were bright, as they had been the night she
and Thorne had argued so bitterly on the terrace. The
moon was full, too, turning the statues in the garden to
silver.

Aimlessly, she walked past the gazebo and through the
hydrangeas beyond.

"To what do I owe this visit?"

Though Thorne's voice cut sharply into the night,
taking her by surprise, she wasn't startled. As before,
when she'd met him on the esplanade, perhaps her
treacherous subconscious had caused her to seek him out.

"You forgot I lived back here?"

"No. I didn't think of it." She slowed still more as he
fell into step beside her. "I'm sorry about what I said to
you in Salem. Accusing you of wanting to get your hands
on Miriam's money. I think your idea of setting up me-

morials to George that will benefit the community is wonderful.''

Why should she leave false accusations hanging between them simply because he chose to do so? Her apology was only meant to put a period at the end of the sentence.

He didn't comment on what she'd said. "I'm sorry I won't be able to take you to the airport in the morning. I have to be in court."

"You've done enough. Kevin is going to drive me."

"I guessed he would. How long will it take to tie things up when you get back to Los Angeles?"

"Tie things up?"

"When will you be back?"

How nice it would have been if his interest in her plans was personal. If he would follow up his question with something about how much he would miss her. How he'd be counting the days, weeks, hours they'd be separated. But rather, it was a case of how much time will I have for a breather, before I have to deal with you again?

"I won't be back in the foreseeable future."

"I assumed from what Miriam said that you had been persuaded to move to Boston."

Addie shook her head. It was news to her that Miriam had been saying that, but she supposed it wasn't really a surprise. Miriam, no doubt, would be delighted to have her move to Boston. "I have a job in Los Angeles. I have family and friends." she said.

"What about your family here?"

His emphasis on the word "family" made the skin prickle at the back of her neck. "As you've pointed out, the family ties I have in Boston are distant ones."

"I see." He didn't believe her.

How could someone with such a sensitive face be so lacking in understanding? He could only imagine one motive for anything she might do. Financial gain. He couldn't visualize her acting out of love, or pride, or caring.

There was nothing more to say. "I'd better get inside. Miriam will wonder about me." She took a step backwards. "If you're ever in Los Angeles..."

"I'll look you up," he finished for her.

The silence was absolute. It could still happen, she thought. He was so close she could feel his warmth. He had only to lean toward her, and she would meet him halfway, for the kiss that would have to last her forever.

"I hope you do," she said tritely. "I'd like to reciprocate all the trouble you've taken with me."

"It was my pleasure." His eyes, as clear and startling as the blue of the evening sky, caressed hers. "I hope you find what you're looking for."

What she was looking for? It was an insinuating phrase under the circumstances. Her face colored with what she knew was a blaze of indignation.

"I will." She widened her eyes suggestively. "We have more than our share of millionaires in California. Oilmen. Movie producers."

"Rock stars," he added, smiling tentatively at her sarcasm.

"One of them is bound to get sick, come to the hospital and—" she snapped her fingers "—happy ever after."

"He'll give you that emerald you want, along with the things that go with it. I almost wish I were in a position to..." Now it was his turn to fumble for words.

The emerald. He still thought...

Maybe in another lifetime. She tossed her head ineffectively. Her freshly shampooed hair felt heavy on her neck.

"I don't imagine we'll be seeing each other again."

"I guess not." He tasted his lower lip.

"Goodbye, then." She turned away hastily, wondering if she could make it to the house without bursting into tears.

"Addie, wait." In answer to her silent prayer, he grasped her shoulders with both hands and pressed his face into her hair. "Don't go yet. I can't let you just disappear from my life. There must be a way we can work this out. I know I've said some terrible things..."

"We both have," she agreed, holding only a small hope that he might actually have had a change of heart.

"God, it seems so long since I've kissed you," he muttered against her ear, sending the remnants of her determination skyward.

Too long, she thought, as silently, he turned her toward him, a fraction of an inch at a time. Kisses didn't lie, the lyrics of love songs insisted. If that was true, when his lips found hers, he would be knocked off his feet by the impact of what she felt for him. He would know that a paper ring from a twenty-five-cent cigar would serve as well as a jewel, if he were to present it to her.

Unexpectedly the patio lights went on, and Kevin appeared on the terrace. "Better get inside," he called. "There's trouble afoot."

At first, Addie supposed something had happened to Miriam. But her aunt was sitting on the couch, apparently well enough, except that she'd been weeping.

"My sapphire necklace has disappeared," she cried, when Addie and Thorne came in.

"Auntie and I were wondering if the clasp should be repaired." Kevin took a drink from the ubiquitous glass he carried. "She opened the chest to look at it, and the necklace wasn't there."

Thorne clapped a hand to the back of his neck. "You were tired the night Addie wore it. Couldn't you have dropped it into another drawer, thinking you'd put it away properly the next day?"

"Absolutely not." Miriam dabbed at her eyes. "I distinctly remember. While Addie was in her tub, I held it for a long time, talking with George about it, wanting to know if he was pleased that it had been worn again. And don't look at me like that, Thorne. I talk to him all the time. It helps me remember the good times. And who can say that the spirits of those we love don't hover around watching over us?"

"Maybe George took it back then," Kevin drawled, heading for the bar. "Well, hell. I told you not to keep something so valuable in the house."

"Wasn't anything else stolen?" Addie asked.

"That's the odd thing about it." Miriam rose stiffly and put an arm around the girl's shoulders. "Why would a burglar bypass the rest of what's in the jewelry drawer and take only the necklace? Why didn't he just scoop it all into his sack, or whatever it is a burglar carries?"

"Sounds like an inside job." Kevin took another healthy drink. "One of the servants saw Auntie put the necklace away and decided that since it was worn so seldom, it might be years before its loss would be discovered."

"No one who works for me would do such a thing," Miriam protested. "They've all been with me for years."

"And they've probably been burning with jealousy the whole time," Kevin said.

"What an unkind thing to say," Miriam scolded.

"Who else could be responsible? You might as well face it, dear. You're going to have to question the servants. The police will."

"Police?" His aunt looked stricken.

"Yes, the police. What do you intend to do?" Kevin drained his glass and reached for the bottle again. "Make the thief a present of your necklace?"

"How dreadful." Miriam gave Addie an apologetic smile. "I'm only sorry it had to happen just before you leave, Adeline. It'll spoil your whole trip."

"Sorry, toots," Kevin said out of the corner of his mouth, flicking the ashes off an imaginary cigar. "Nobody goes anywhere, until the perpetrator is caught."

"Kevin!" Miriam cried out, shocked.

"The first thing the police are going to want to know is who was here," Kevin continued. "For my own peace of mind, I insist on having my room searched."

"No," Miriam moaned, catching Thorne's arm for support.

"Yes. And there's no time like the present. Come along. I want you all as witnesses." Except for Kevin, everyone was silent as they filed upstairs. "I think I've seen this movie before," he said, grinning as if it was all a joke. "Agatha Christie, wasn't it?"

"I think you've had too much to drink," Miriam berated him as, once in his room, he systematically opened one dresser drawer after another. "I'm appalled by all this."

"It doesn't matter," Addie said, squeezing her aunt's hand. "It's only a formality. It doesn't mean anything."

"I know this doesn't exonerate me," Kevin went on, when the search had been completed. "There's still my getaway car. Cameron can do the honors. He'll need

some tools, won't you, old boy? To take off the panel-
ing and the hubcaps. That'll come later, though. For
now, I guess it's Addie's turn. Want to lead the way, little cousin?''

"You're going too far," Miriam cried, throwing herself into Addie's path. "I won't have it,''

"Very well." Kevin shrugged. "But I imagine Addie
would feel better if she got the same treatment the rest of
us did.''

Addie touched a hand gently to her aunt's shoulder. "I
wouldn't want to be the exception.''

Like a house detective used to conducting such
searches, Kevin hummed the theme of one of the prime-
time TV detective series as he opened drawers and went
through the pockets of the garments hanging in Addie's
closet. He even threw back the mattress before he was
satisfied.

"You're in the clear, girlie," he drawled, Humphrey
Bogart style. "Unless you had an accomplice waiting
outside your window and passed it to him." He looked
pointedly at Thorne. "And maybe a fence in Salem?''

"May we go back now and sit down?" Miriam begged.

"Why not?" Absently, Kevin pulled a suitcase from
under the bed as an afterthought and opened it. "You
haven't started to pack yet?" he asked Addie.

All that was in the case was a pair of rain boots. Addie hadn't bothered to take them out. The weather had
been dry, except for the unexpected storm in Salem.
Kevin lifted one and dropped it, then picked up the other
and frowned. After shaking it, he cast a puzzled look at
her and turned the boot over.

Something fell onto the carpet. To Addie's astonish-
ment it was the sapphire necklace, wrapped in a paisley
scarf.

"It...it isn't possible," she whispered. "How did it get there?"

"George maybe?" Kevin snorted. "In a generous mood?"

"I didn't put it there," she insisted, unable to take her eyes off the necklace. "Truly, I didn't."

"No one thinks you did, darling," Miriam said uncertainly. "Perhaps I didn't put it back, after all. Perhaps I left it on the dresser and when you were thinking of what to pack, you accidentally..."

"Accidentally wrapped it in a scarf and stuck it in the toe of your boot," Kevin broke in with an ugly smile.

"The important thing is that you found it," Thorne said in a tight voice unlike his own.

"Miriam, the last time I saw that necklace was when you unfastened the clasp and took it into your room," Addie went on, though her insistence sounded false even to her own ears. "Someone else must have put it with my things."

"It doesn't matter. I intended to give it to you, anyway." Miriam's tone was too bright.

"Sorry about this, Cameron." Kevin slapped the other man's shoulder. "Now you won't get to interrogate the servants."

Sporadic conversation continued, as the group straggled back into the living room. No one mentioned the necklace again, but the subject hung over the room like a black cloud. Miriam talked about how much she would miss her niece. Kevin talked about when they should leave to get to the airport in plenty of time.

Addie didn't try again to protest her innocence. No one would have believed her. Not Thorne, judging by the way he'd avoided her eyes since the necklace had been discovered. Not even Miriam, who was trying too hard to make excuses for her.

Only one person knew she wasn't guilty. The person who had planted the necklace in her boot as a bit of extra insurance.

Her loving cousin, Kevin.

CHAPTER THIRTEEN

ADDIE WAS GREETED, on her return from Boston, by the balmy sort of weather promised to Southern California tourists. It was weather that had, as always, brought Barney home with a collection of bright-colored seed packets and a spiel about the joys of homegrown vegetables.

The work on her desk had piled up higher than the junk mail that awaited her half-hearted perusal at home, and she welcomed it. The busier she was, the sooner she'd drop back into her old routine.

She and Frank began to meet often for lunch. They went to a new exhibit at the Art Museum and attended a mime performance at a little theater on Melrose Avenue. Despite her feverish attempts to capture life as it had been before Thorne, a part of her remained in Massachusetts.

Miriam wrote regularly with news of an unseasonable warm spell and of Thorne's victories in court and in the boardroom. She also mentioned an accident Kevin had while drinking that resulted in a bent fender, a broken wrist and suspension of his driver's license.

"I hope by now you've forgiven him for his wickedness toward you," she'd written, evidently having found out somehow about the pass Kevin had made at Addie in his apartment that day. "He's a darling boy, really, and only behaves badly when he's under the influence. I think, too, he's been upset by not being allowed enough

authority. An opportunity has come up in our Paris office, and he's eager to go. There'll be problems with some
of the board members who've heard negative things
about him, but the work he's done lately has proved him
very capable. I've agreed to back him all the way, *if* he
agrees to get help. I understand they have excellent pro-
grams for alcoholics."

Miriam, who saw everyone and everything through a
rosy haze of affection, had probably also managed to
convince herself that her necklace had found its way into
her niece's luggage by some innocent means.

When everyone had left that terrible last evening, and
Addie had tried to talk about the necklace, Miriam had
brushed it off as unimportant.

"What's past is past."

So all was forgiven **and** soon to be forgotten. Except
that she didn't want to be forgiven for something she
didn't do, not by Miriam, and certainly not by Thorne.

There'd been a phone call too, as well as the letters.
Miriam was opening the house at Cape Cod and hoped
Addie might spend the summer with her.

"Bring your grandfather with you this time. I can't see
how a few hours of flight would hurt. And I'm dying to
meet him. Especially now that he and I are partners, so
to speak."

Addie's refusal was regretful but firm. Her own letters were as friendly and chatty as they had always been.
They were briefer, however, and less frequent. In time,
the older woman's need for her company would fade.

Friday night meant poker for Barney and his cronies
again. The games had stopped for a time. He hadn't the
heart for them when he was worried about keeping the
hardware store. Now with those concerns put to rest by
the new loan arrangements, and with his enthusiasm for

business revived by Cousin Miriam's involvement, even at a distance, it was back to his comfortable old routine.

To Addie's relief, that evening's game was being held at the home of one of the other players. She usually didn't mind Barney's poker nights, but right now she wasn't in the mood for the inevitable hoots and clatter, the smoke and shuffling around the house that accompanied them.

"I'm getting to be a real bear," she acknowledged, as she found herself welcoming the prospect of a quiet evening to herself.

As penance for her new antisocial thoughts, she decided to clear out the hall closet. It was a hopeless jumble of things that were never used. With Barney gone for the evening, she could pitch things out and not worry about his rushing in to rescue a sweater with an unraveled sleeve or a battered fishing hat he hadn't worn in fifteen years.

She'd stopped at the drugstore on her way home from the hospital and picked up two cardboard boxes from their trash. She'd pack them and call the Veterans' Thrift Shop the next morning to arrange for a pickup.

Certain it was Frank when the telephone jangled, she balanced the box of old shoes she was carrying on one hip, snatched up the receiver and answered with a breathless "Yes?"

"Addie?"

Allowing the box to slide to the floor, she thrust the phone away and stared at it for a long moment.

"Who is this?" she stammered. As if she didn't know.

"It's Thorne. Addie? Are you there?"

"I'm just surprised to hear from you," she began. Then the most obvious reason for his call struck her and she sucked in her breath. "Is Miriam all right?"

"She's fine. I'd like to take you up on your offer. To show me the sights of LA. Remember? You were serious, weren't you?"

"Yes. Of course." She lowered herself into a chair with the concentration of someone who wasn't sure if it would be pulled out from under her. As it was, the telephone had probably picked up and magnified the bongo-drum beating of her heart. "When will you be here? If I know in plenty of time, I can arrange theater tickets."

"I'm not sure. Wait." In the background was the roar of traffic as though he was calling from a pay phone. "I'm at the intersection of Sepulveda and Santa Monica," he said. "As far as I can tell from the street map I picked up at the airport, I should be able to drive to your house in, uh, ten minutes."

Panic swept through her as she resisted the impulse to hang up. "You're in town? *Now?*"

"Is it a bad time for you?"

Yes, yes, yes. Go away.

"Not at all," she answered weakly. "It's just that— why didn't you let me know you were coming?"

"It came up unexpectedly. I tried to get you last night."

She and Barney had gone to the movies. "We were out."

"If it's inconvenient—"

"No. It's fine. I'll expect you in ten minutes, then."

"Give or take a few."

She wasted one of those minutes staring at her image in the mirror, wondering if the three pounds she'd gained since her return from Boston showed. She wasted another, juggling two possibilities. Should she straighten the living room so it wouldn't appear she was living in a junk shop, or should she make herself presentable?

The situation called for both. First she crammed every thing she could back into the closet, allowing a pathway, at least, from door to couch. Then she raced to the bedroom with a groan, feeling not unlike a contestant in a nightmarish quiz show, trying to beat the clock and avoid the hideous consequence.

Off came her jeans and Morris the Cat T-shirt. On went her cream silk shirt and beige linen skirt.

Resisting the impulse to squander the seconds it took to look out the window, she began to brush her hair furiously. When, predictably, it refused to fall smoothly to her shoulders, she gathered it atop her head into a tousle of jaunty curls like a nineteenth-century coquette, and fastened it with a green beribboned clip.

Maybe Thorne would misread the map, take a wrong turn and end up in Century City. He'd call apologetically and say he was on the corner of one street or another and ask for directions. That would give her time for mascara, eyeshadow—the works.

But of course that wouldn't happen. He'd never been lost in his life. A dusting of powder on her nose and a hasty application of coral lipstick would have to serve. Off came her sneakers and on went the new taupe sandals with the spindly heels that did so much for her legs. And there was the doorbell.

The long weeks of separation had worked no magic cures. They hadn't even begun to dull the impact of that first moment she opened the door and Thorne's gaze collided with hers.

"Hello, Addie."

How was his flight, she recited, and was he exhausted? Had he seen a movie? He apologized for giving no notice of his arrival and she assured him he wasn't intruding. Then they just stood there looking at each other.

He wore a black shirt with a silky sheen, the gray jacket she remembered, and dark slacks. Though he looked travel-weary, he also looked incredibly appealing.

"May I sit down?"

"If you can find a place," she said, trying too hard to be breezy. "Barney's out for the evening and I'm cleaning house. Things have to look worse before they can look better."

He nodded gravely, as if he understood, shifted a box of paperback westerns from the couch to the floor and motioned for her to sit beside him.

"It's after six." She looked at the clock, hoping to break the hypnotic effect of his gaze. "Too late to do anything tonight in the way of sight-seeing. I don't work tomorrow, though, and if you'd tell me where your interests lie, I'll—"

"Could we have dinner somewhere? You haven't eaten yet, have you?"

The invitation was a welcome one. All at once the room was too small and too cozy. She needed larger, less intimate surroundings to divorce herself from her feelings, from how terribly she'd missed him. The Hollywood Bowl, for instance.

"I could fix something for us here."

"I came a long way to see you, and need more than a fraction of your attention, which is all you'd be able to give me if you're scurrying around a cluttered kitchen."

"Some of us don't make clutter when we cook," she teased.

A corner of his mouth twitched to make way for a beguiling smile. "You'll have to teach me your secret. But not tonight. I want that talk we owe each other." He hadn't touched her yet. He hadn't even grasped her hand in greeting. Yet she felt as though she'd been on the receiving end of an unsettling caress.

"Have we ever done that? Talked, I mean?"

"Not often." The fleeting smile came again. "But those times were shining ones."

Yes, they were, she almost answered. But then, she remembered, and certainly he did, too. Those shining times were too often overshadowed by the other, darker ones.

Absently, he reached for a piece of the puzzle Barney had spread out on the coffee table and tried to fit it into the wrong place. She resisted the impulse to correct him.

"The picture is a hamburger?" he asked.

She lifted one shoulder. "There aren't many things these days that haven't been used for one of these puzzles."

"I know a place not far from here I think you'll like," he said, abandoning his efforts. "The food is excellent, the service is good and the waiters don't hover. Shall we go?"

"Something's wrong here, Mr. Cameron. I'm supposed to be showing you the city."

"I have a confession to make." He looked past her toward the kitchen, where the refrigerator had begun to chug noisily.

"You've been to LA before and know it as well as I do," she accused.

"I wouldn't say that—exactly."

"Why did you pretend—"

"I'm ravenous," he interrupted, standing up and holding out a hand to her. "What do you say we argue about this over dinner?"

Dinner was Fisherman's Platter, with every kind of seafood imaginable on the sizzling metal tray. It was so delicious and she was so pleased about being with Thorne again, she couldn't bring herself to destroy the mood by raking over obvious conflicts. Instead, she permitted herself to revel in listening to his voice and watching him eat and drink, though she didn't go so far as to allow her eyes the luxury of lingering on his full, perfectly formed mouth.

His hair was shorter than it had been when she saw him last, and she wondered how the sensible woman she'd always considered herself to be could possibly be moved by the thought of a man—any man—simply having a new haircut.

Through the meal, their conversation was light, about his work and hers, all the things people discussed who'd been apart only a few days. It would grow serious, though, she knew, and when it did, she saw it coming.

Looking uncomfortable, he cleared his throat and rested his hands on the table in the manner of a judge who'd come to a difficult decision.

"I want you to come back to Boston, Addie. For the summer, at least."

She'd taken a sip of coffee, swallowed too quickly, and couldn't answer immediately. The delay gave truth the time it needed to register. "Do you really have business in LA, Thorne?" she asked. "Or am I that business?"

"You know me too well."

"Are you sure you'd want to chance having me as Miriam's houseguest again? I might make another try for the necklace."

A breaded shrimp stopped an inch from his mouth and moved down to his plate again. "What's that?"

"Don't tell me you've forgotten about my trying to make off with the sapphire necklace."

"It seems you haven't forgotten."

"How could I? The way you—the way everyone—looked at me. I've never been so humiliated."

"It happened so suddenly. No one had time to think."

"Or to consider that I might be innocent. That someone else might have put that necklace in my suitcase to make me look bad."

Thorne put down his fork and reached across the table for her hand, but she saw it coming and pulled away. "Miriam told me it was all settled. That you understood."

"How could it be settled? Kevin wanted me to leave under a shadow and he accomplished it."

"I wouldn't say that. Miriam's wise to his tricks. She suspected from the first what he'd done, but couldn't prove it. Then one night, when he'd been drinking heavily, she made him confess. She said she wrote to you about it."

"She didn't." Or did she?

When Miriam had written about Addie's forgiving Kevin's wickedness toward her, she'd assumed her aunt was talking about the way he'd behaved in his apartment. But maybe she'd been referring to the necklace.

"She never imagined you were guilty. She thought you knew that."

"You imagined I was, though, didn't you?"

"Not after the initial shock wore off. After all, why should you bother to steal a necklace when it will probably be yours, anyway—that and a great deal more?"

Addie pressed her lips together and blew out her cheeks. As usual, Thorne had picked her up with one hand and knocked her down with the other. The two of them were back to square one.

"Miriam's health is failing," he went on. "She has a weak heart and borderline diabetes. It's important she take proper care of herself."

"I know that."

"I was wrong to make things difficult for you. Whatever your motives for stepping into the family circle, Miriam needs you. Your place is with her."

Whatever your motives. Whatever your motives. The phrase was the same one he'd used just before they'd called their short-lived truce in front of the Minuteman statue. Well, she'd warned him that day what would happen if he ever did it again. If he ever put her off guard, then threw his insults at her, reminding her that she was a pretender.

She'd sloshed some of her coffee onto the table when she set her cup down. The stain was spreading, dark and ugly on the white cloth. It reminded her of a scene in a vintage World War II movie she and Barney had watched on TV. Insulted by the leering enemy general, the heroine had hurled a cup of coffee in his face. "Swine!" she'd hissed.

Addie saw herself snatching up her own cup and tossing its contents in Thorne's face. She could visualize his astonished reaction, the snickering of the other patrons.

"Would you excuse me, please?" she asked with surprising amiability. "No, don't get up." She waved him back into his chair and retreated to the powder room.

Once out of sight, she dug into her handbag for her notepad and a ballpoint pen. She tore off a sheet of paper and scribbled hurriedly.

"I meant what I said in Lexington," she wrote. "Now I'm taking a cab home. Stay away from me. Addie."

The woman at the cash register only nodded when Addie handed her the square of folded paper and asked her to wait five minutes before delivering it to the man in the black shirt at the far table. Evidently what she was doing wasn't all that uncommon.

A vine-covered divider hid her departure, and she sped out of the restaurant to find herself swallowed by an eerie white fog. It was one of the things she disliked about living so near the ocean. But she welcomed it now. It made escape easier.

CHAPTER FOURTEEN

A REVIVAL THEATER a block away was showing *Casablanca,* a movie Addie had seen more times than she could count. Still, it offered sanctuary until she was sure Thorne had gone and she could call a taxi and go home. And if she were to cry in that darkened auditorium, people around her would suppose her tears were for Bogart and Bergman's ill-fated love, not her own.

She didn't cry, though. By the time she left the theater with the rest of the audience, she'd come to a decision, as the characters had in the movie.

Barney was home, she noticed as she paid her cab fare. His coddled fifteen-year-old Chevy was in its place and covered with its protective tarp. That was good. He'd guess that something was wrong, but he wouldn't ask. They'd share a pot of hot chocolate. He'd tell her the highlights of his poker game and how he'd bluffed his way through a "nothing" hand, and before long, he'd make her laugh, as he'd always been able to do when she was younger.

The key stuck in the lock as usual, and she had to jiggle it to make it work. As she did, she paused, wondering at the sound of voices. Who had Barney invited home with him?

With a sigh of resignation, she let herself in, prepared to play enthusiastic hostess for her grandfather's sake.

Her smile faded before it began. The guest wasn't one of Barney's cronies. It was Thorne.

He was seated on the couch, knee-deep in photo albums. He'd removed his jacket. His shirt adhered cleanly to the arousing lines of his chest and shoulders. The disarming smile he offered might be expected, she thought morosely. It went with his job. But attorneys weren't supposed to be so devilishly attractive.

"You're home early," she said to Barney lightly, as if Thorne's presence was immaterial. "What happened? Did you lose all your money?"

"As a matter of fact, I'm six bucks to the good," her grandfather assured her. "But all the weeding I did in the vegetable patch did me in." He stretched himself into a standing position, tested his knees and pressed a hand to the small of his back. "Now that you're here to do your own entertaining, I'll hit the hay."

She took a quick step toward him. "Don't you want your hot chocolate?"

"I need my rest more." Either not noticing, or ignoring her pleading expression, he thrust out a hand to Thorne. "Enjoyed meeting you, Cameron. You know where we live now. Don't be a stranger. We'll talk about those Camerons I knew when I lived in Ojai. I've got some pictures somewhere. If you're lucky, we might find a matchup."

"It's easy to see where you got your interest in photography," Thorne said when they were alone, looking somewhat overwhelmed. "I've never seen so many pictures."

"It serves you right if you were bored."

"I didn't say I was bored. Not at all. I saw you at six days old, six weeks, six months. We'd gone through two albums before you reached your second birthday. Then

there was your sister, your brother, your mother and father..."

Addie pressed her lips together to suppress a smile.
"Why are you here?"

"I had to make sure you got home all right."

"I did, as you can see." She set her handbag on the hall
tree and turned her back to him, not caring that the fog
had taken every bit of curl out of her hair. This time she
wouldn't allow her disheveled appearance to befuddle
her.

"I saw all the family research you did, too." Idly he
picked up one of several manila folders that lay on top of
a box at his feet. "So much of the writing in these old
documents is blurry to the point of being indecipher-
able. I can imagine how many hours you put into it."

"No, you can't," she said, brushing aside his attempts at flattery.

"You only made the trip to Boston because of your
grandfather's coaxing. He told me."

"In other words, he was a corroborating witness." She
folded her arms and stared at him blankly. "What are
you getting at?"

"I was surprised you didn't tell him about Miriam's
money."

That *would* surprise him, she thought. "I *did* tell him.
At least about Miriam's connection with Mandeville
Chocolates. I don't suppose he thought it was that im-
portant."

"He suggested that if she misses you so much, she
should put her house up for sale and come to live here.
She could have the guest bedroom."

His grin stirred the embers of her outrage again.
"Would that be so ridiculous? It's a comfortable room."

He sobered quickly. "I didn't mean—"

"Yes, you did."

"Not the way it sounded."

"Exactly the way it sounded." The refrigerator began to chug again, louder this time than she'd ever heard it before. Barney was running water in the bathroom and the hot-water pipes were rattling. It was a far cry from hearing Harry James in the background at Thorne's apartment. She had an impulse to laugh, and yet, at the same time, she wanted to cry.

"You told him about the securities," Thorne said. "I didn't think you would."

"I didn't think I would, either. I was afraid it would hurt his pride." She shook her head. "But after all the intrigue I saw in Boston, the lies stacked one on top of the other, I had no choice."

Thorne smiled. "He told me it only went to prove how family sticks together in a crisis. That he planned on paying Miriam a percentage until the loan is paid in full, and he wouldn't hear any arguments that it wasn't coming out of her pocket."

"It's getting late," Addie said. "I appreciate your dropping in, but..."

"You want me to go." He slapped his hands on his knees and stood up.

Her fingers flew to the top button of her blouse in panic as he moved toward her, but then she realized he had to pass her to to get to the door. "Don't forget your jacket."

If he heard her, he didn't react. "Barney is everything you told me he was," he said, coming to a stop directly in front of her. He was close enough that she had to tilt her chin to look into his face. "I like him."

Barney liked Thorne, too. It was evident from the way he'd gone to bed to give them a chance to be alone. It was something he'd never done with anyone. Not even with Frank. Especially not with Frank.

"Thank you," she said, leaving it at that.

She almost reminded him of his jacket again, but didn't. That would be pushing too hard.

"I was wrong about you, Addie," he admitted. "Right from the beginning."

"You feel that way because of the things Barney told you?"

"Yes. No. I suppose I knew the person you were all along. I just didn't know how to accept the truth. I'm sorry."

"No harm done," she said softly. No harm done? Only her previously smooth-running life turned upside down. Her hopes and dreams for the future shattered.

Fumbling for the right words, Thorne went on, trying to explain again how he had, through his lifetime, come into contact with so many greedy self-serving people, he'd forgotten how to trust.

"You couldn't possibly have feigned your affection for Miriam," he said. "Or your frankness and openhearted innocence, any more than your grandfather could have feigned his love of family and jigsaw puzzles. I guess I deserve to lose you. But Miriam doesn't. It's too bad."

Bent on keeping intact the shell she'd built around herself, Addie forced her thoughts elsewhere. To the eggs she needed for breakfast in the morning and had forgotten to buy. To her job and the unpleasant task she'd been assigned—to terminate the employment of a newcomer who'd been disrupting hospital routine. She'd never had to fire anyone before; how would she go about it? To the jet black of Thorne's shirt that echoed the blackness of his hair. To the sweep of his lashes, also black, and the ever-changing color of his eyes.

When had he moved so close? Was he counting on proximity to accomplish what his words hadn't? Would it help if she were to recite the alphabet backwards? Or Hamlet's soliloquy?

"I should have taken you to the airport," he said suddenly, probably guessing that she wasn't listening.

"In Boston, you mean?" She blinked, confused by the change of subjects. "It wasn't your fault if you had to be in court that day."

"I didn't," he confessed. "I was holed up in my apartment, hoping that when you were gone, what I was feeling for you would be gone, too."

She nodded, remembering her own relief that he hadn't been there for her goodbyes.

"I missed out on my goodbye kiss."

Was he always chalking up missed kisses, like unpaid bills, to be collected at a more prudent time?

"As I recall, we weren't on kissing terms then."

"Would you mind if I take it now? I came a long way to get it."

"You flew to LA for a kiss, I suppose."

"In a way, I did. It's true what I said about Miriam's wanting you. But I'm the one who needs you. You're what's been missing from my life. I've only been marking time since you left."

His kiss was the last thing she needed. It was the key that opened the door to a room from which she'd just escaped. A room full of dark corners and uncertainties. On the other hand, if she refused, he'd believe he'd won.

She didn't flinch as he edged closer still, but her breathing was wrong. "A kiss wouldn't prove anything," she said, her voice breaking on the word "kiss."

Taking her answer as assent, he caught her around the waist in a way that had become familiar to her. At the same time, his free hand found a place between her shoulder blades, his fingers splayed and pressing.

"I'm not out to prove anything," he said. "Are you?"

"Of course not." She looked at him stolidly. At least, she hoped she did.

His hands shifted at her back, smoothing, caressing, heating her skin. Her color would be high, she knew, as if she'd been in the sun too long.

"I came to a decision tonight after I left you." She pulled back just as he leaned toward her.

His mouth missed its mark and caught her ear, scalding it, filling her with unexpected pleasure. "What decision is that?" he muttered, testing her lobe with the edge of his teeth.

"I plan to write Miriam as often as I like," she said, turning again, so that his lips scorched a burning trail across her cheek. "I'll call her if I like, too, and visit whenever I choose. Next time I'll take Barney with me. He'd probably enjoy seeing Paul Revere's house."

"I doubt it. Unless Revere was in your family tree."

"I'm serious."

"I know you are." His mouth hovered over the side of her neck, numbing her protective instincts as he prepared for a new assault.

"Why should I hurt Miriam and deprive myself of her affection and friendship only to humor you?" she cried, her voice shrill, as a tremor rolled through her.

"Why, indeed?" When she moved this time, he was ready. The hand at her lower back pressed harder to compensate, and the other flew up to catch her chin and hold it firmly in place.

Her moan of frustration turned to a blissful sigh as she gratefully accepted his lips.

He'd asked for only one kiss, but took two, three, four, greedily, until her ability to argue or reason deserted her. "In fact, if I have my way, when you go back to Boston, it won't be for a visit. It'll be to stay."

She tilted her head back, better to search his eyes. "What do you mean?"

"You know very well what I mean. We're perfect together. Like pieces in one of your grandfather's puzzles."

She shook her head. "We have too many problems."

"So? When pieces of a puzzle belong together," he argued, "you work with them until they fall into place."

"If you have to struggle to put them together, they don't fit."

"Then the analogy is wrong."

"Is it?"

"Name one problem we have that can't be solved by two people who love each other." He thought for a moment. "Conflicting careers?"

"No, no." She brushed aside his suggestion. "I'm flexible about that, even if you're not."

"Geographical preference?"

"No. At least, that wouldn't be a problem with me."

"Fine. And you can't put the blame on Barney. Much as he likes Los Angeles, he told me that being open to change and willing to make new friends keeps a man young."

"You've already discussed this with him?" she asked, surprised.

"Why not? Your father isn't here. I can't ask him for your hand, the way Abner and Jeremiah did when they were young."

"Ezekiel and Isaiah," she corrected, blinking back the tears that stung her eyes.

"So, it had to be Barney. Besides, it'll take a lot of work to start up a business in a new location. He's affected by any decision you make, isn't he?"

"Yes, but—"

"Then where are those insurmountable problems you mentioned?"

How could she say it without making it sound like an accusation? How could she explain her fear of being hurt again, as only he could hurt her? "I can't be sure of you from one minute to the next. You're so...changeable."

"Granted. But you were wrong, too. You might have tried to see things from my point of view. Your arriving when you did, almost immediately after those articles about Miriam in the magazines. You might have had more patience with me and given me a chance to discover the truth."

"I might have," she agreed grudgingly.

"It only took a few words to make you fly off the handle at me."

"Maybe."

"As for my changing, it'll never happen. Not where you're concerned. I can't put my finger on the exact moment I admitted to myself that I love you."

"Admitted to yourself?" she questioned.

"Yes. Admitted. Look for an insult in that, if you will. But if you're honest with yourself, the same thing applies to your willingness to admit you're in love with me."

"Maybe," she said again, remembering the force field of antagonism that had existed between her and Thorne in those first, often dreadful, meetings.

"Even through the bitterest of our battles I couldn't deny how very special you were to me. How very special you would always be. I want us to be married as quickly as possible. I don't care if it's here in your living room or in the most elegant church in Boston.'' His eyes swept her face briefly, before he kissed her again, soundly, lovingly, possessively. ''Doesn't that tell you something?''

She swallowed hard. ''You can't read kisses the way you read palms.''

His grin was impish. ''But it's fun trying.''

Why did she believe him?

As he'd said, the pieces of the gigantic puzzle they'd made of their relationship had fallen securely into place. The arms that held her now were the only ones she would ever want to hold her. The lips that had just taken hers were the only ones she would ever need.

Why was she doing all this soul-searching and arguing inside herself? She had no intention of sending him away. ''How do I know you don't want me for my money?'' she teased.

He pulled back, one eyebrow lifted questioningly. ''How can I prove my intentions are honorable?''

''I don't know.'' The argument was over. The evidence had been presented, but she wanted to make the moment last a bit longer before she read the final verdict. Twining her arms around his neck, she held him fast, the way she planned to hold him always. ''You'll have to be put through some rigorous testing.''

Standing on tiptoe, she pressed her lips to one of his cheekbones. Then for balance, she pressed them to the other.

How wonderful it was going to be. To feel free to do whatever she liked with Thorne—whenever she liked. How wonderful, too, to allow him the same privilege.

''Is that a sample of the testing you plan to put me through?'' His voice was thick with ill-concealed urgency.

"It is," she answered, trying to sound stern.

His hands moved at her back again, as he leaned down to meet her kiss halfway. "Then let's get on with it," he said.

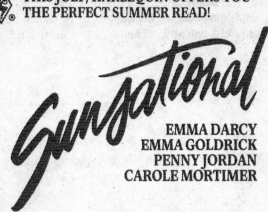